CONCANNON

**Center Point
Large Print**

**This Large Print Book carries the
Seal of Approval of N.A.V.H.**

CONCANNON

CLIFTON ADAMS

CENTER POINT PUBLISHING
THORNDIKE, MAINE

This Center Point Large Print edition
is published in the year 2005 by arrangement with
Golden West Literary Agency.

Copyright © 1972 by Geraldine F. Adams as Administratrix
for the Estate of Clifton H. Adams.

The text of this Large Print edition is unabridged. In other
aspects, this book may vary from the original edition. Printed in
Thailand. Set in 16-point Times New Roman type.

ISBN 1-58547-635-8

Library of Congress Cataloging-in-Publication Data

Adams, Clifton.
    Concannon / Clifton Adams.--Center Point large print ed.
        p. cm.
    ISBN 1-58547-635-8 (lib. bdg. : alk. paper)
    1. Large type books. I. Title.

PS3551.D34C66 2005
813'.54--dc22

                                                        2005003938

CHAPTER 1

John Evers, the division inspector, was waiting in front of the Santa Fe depot when Concannon dropped out of the express car. The inspector came forward, smiling, his hand held out to be shaken. "Welcome to Oklahoma City. She's changed some since we first laid track through here in '87."

They shook hands briefly. Evers was a large, trim man who looked as though he had never been late for a meal or slept in an uncomfortable bed. Despite his appearance, he was known to be shrewd, ruthless, one of the best railroad agents in the business. Concannon had never liked him much.

They walked leisurely along the siding, ignoring the huffing and clamor of the big Baldwin, dodging baggage and mail carts, picking their way through the raucous confusion of disembarking passengers, and the inevitable congregation of loafers. "I'm a little pressed for time," Evers said, smiling blandly. "Got to catch the stagecoach to Fort Sill in about twenty minutes, but we'll have time enough to talk. Did they tell you anything in Arkansas City?"

"Just that Allard's dead, and there's a big company loss."

"Big loss is right. Hundred thousand dollars, thereabouts."

Concannon followed the inspector into the depot. A hundred thousand dollars—the robbers must be enjoying themselves. Dancing on Allard's grave.

The ticket agent saw them coming and quickly unlocked the door and let them into a small office. "This here's Mr. Concannon, Sam," Evers smiled to the agent. "He's come all the way down from Wichita to do a job of work for us. Help him any way you can."

They went on into the office without waiting to hear what the agent might reply. It was a naked box of a room, with a yellow oak desk and two chairs and a big Santa Fe calendar on the wall. The furniture was coated with a light layer of soot and grit. It was exactly like a hundred other offices that Concannon had been in during the five years that he had worked for the railroad.

Evers gazed into space for a moment. Absently, he drew a leather cigar wallet from an inside pocket and selected a green Cuban. "I seem to recollect that you and Ray Allard were pals once."

It was well known that Concannon and Allard had been friends during the years they had both ridden for the Parker court at Fort Smith. For the past five years they had taken separate trails, but that didn't alter the friendship of half a lifetime. And it didn't make Allard's death any easier for Concannon to accept. It was on Concannon's recommendation that Allard had been hired to ride shotgun on special express shipments—because of that recommendation, Ray Allard was now dead.

But Evers knew all of that. Evers knew everything there was to know about all of his agents.

"We were pals," Concannon said.

"But you didn't see much of one another over the past few years."

"When Ray stopped ridin' for the court at Fort Smith he took a job with a cattlemen's association in Texas. I went to work for the railroad."

"How long did he work for the cattle outfit?"

"A year. Maybe a little longer. Then he took a job as a deputy sheriff, somewhere in Texas. About a year ago he was hired as city marshal in Ellsworth."

Evers looked mildly impressed. "Why did he want to ride shotgun for the railroad when he could be marshal of Ellsworth?"

Concannon shrugged. "He wanted to get married, and he needed the extra money he could get ridin' guard on valuable express shipments."

Evers started to put away his cigar wallet, then, with obvious reluctance, offered one to Concannon.

Concannon accepted it immediately. "Much obliged. What's the reason for all these questions about Allard? I thought you'd be more interested in the men who killed him and stole your hundred thousand dollars."

Evers smiled a bit grimly as he put away his remaining cigars. "You know the answer to that, Concannon. When the railroad loses a valuable shipment, the first man they suspect is the man riding shotgun."

"Even when he gets himself killed protecting company property?"

"Even then. You know the rules. There has to be an investigation." With a silver cutter, Evers clipped the sealed tip of his cigar and meticulously lit it. "I'll tell you

7

what I know about the robbery. It won't take long, but we might as well make ourselves comfortable."

Evers took his rightful place behind the desk and Concannon took the straight oak chair opposite him, quietly admiring his Cuban cigar. It seemed a shame to spoil the perfection of that dappled-green wrapper by putting a match to it.

"Do you know that stretch of track where the robbery took place?" the inspector asked.

"In the Chickasaw Nation. About ten miles north of the Red. A defile between two hills—I know the place."

Evers nodded and then told the railroad's side of the story, in his own detached, impersonal, and dust-dry fashion.

The object of the robbery had been one hundred thousand dollars in grass money—money that Texas cattlemen paid to the Plains tribes for the privilege of grazing their herds on Indian land. At Oklahoma City the money was to have been transferred to the care of the military and turned over to the agent at Darlington. But the money didn't get within a hundred miles of Oklahoma City.

The robbers—there had been four of them—had rolled a boulder onto the track, stopping the train. There had been a brief but violent fight in which the mail clerk and Ray Allard, the special express agent, had been killed. Two of the robbers then kept guard on the train's crew and passengers, while the other two blew open the company safe with a powerful explosive.

"That's something that might be worth looking into,"

Evers said. "The explosive, according to a Texas agent, was nitroglycerin. Powerful enough to blow open a safe, but dangerous to work with, even for an expert. One of the robbers is probably an oilfield worker; either a well shooter or a nitroglycerin hauler."

That was about all there was to it. By the time a special repair crew reached the train and got it started again, the criminals were many miles away, the company was out one hundred thousand dollars, and two men were dead.

Evers winced slightly as Concannon suddenly bit off the end of the cigar and lit it with a flaring sulphur match. "An oilfield worker."

Evers spread his hands and shrugged. "It's only a guess."

"Is that all?"

"There's Ray Allard's widow. I talked to her, once, briefly." His cheeks colored the slightest bit. "All the newspapermen were after her, of course, right after the robbery. She wasn't in much of a mood for talking. Do you know where to find her?"

Concannon shook his head, and Evers said, "The Fine and Dandy Cafe. That's over on Robinson Street, next to Main. She was off for a few days—on account of buryin' her husband, I guess. But she's back on the job now. Do you know her?"

"No. Ray was in Texas when he married; I was on a job up north."

"Athena Allard . . ." Evers allowed himself a small smile. "Well, you'll see about her when you talk to her."

9

"Is it necessary to bother her now, so soon after what happened to Ray?"

"Of course it's necessary. That's your job, bothering people. Worrying and aggravating them until their guard comes down and they blurt out something that you can use against them. That's what it means to be an agent for the railroad."

Concannon smoked his cigar quietly. "Does the company figure there's somethin' we can use against Mrs. Allard, if I can worry it out of her?"

"Anything's possible. As you know. All we're sure about is that a hundred thousand dollars is missing, and that Athena Allard is in the picture somehow. Even if it is only as the widow of the man who was killed in trying to save it for us. Whatever it is, we want to know about it." He looked up at the ceiling and added quietly, "About that hundred thousand dollars. The company wants it back. So do I. Neither one of us is going to be happy until you find it for us."

"If I find it, will there be a bonus in it for me?"

Evers smiled brightly. This was the kind of question that he understood and approved of. "Don't you fret about that. You find the money and the railroad will be fair."

The fair thing, according to the reckoning of railroads, usually amounted to a silver watch and a hearty handshake from the division superintendent. But Concannon let it pass.

Evers rose up from the desk and brushed an imaginary ash from his vest. "If you need any help, you know what to do. The chief of police and the county sheriff will cooperate, if you need them. If the situation should flow over onto Indian land, United States marshals and the military stand ready to give any assistance necessary."

Evers made it sound so easy. If you got into trouble just snap your fingers and there'd be a troop of cavalry and a posse of United States deputies ready to bail you out. But Concannon only nodded. "All right." They shook hands again, briefly, and the inspector walked briskly out of the office, leaving an aroma of expensive cigars and lavender cologne behind him.

Concannon stood for some time on the white chat siding, looking at the town with a jaded eye. Less than five years ago it had been a one-room depot known as Oklahoma Station; now it was a milling conglomeration of brick buildings and canvas-covered shacks, of saloons and churches and schools and businesses. It sprawled in the once lush valley of the Canadian River, churning it to a mass of reddish dust which, in the spring, would be a sea of red clay mud. On this mild October day of 1893, Oklahoma City counted itself exactly four years, three months and five days old—not many cities could reckon their age so precisely.

Concannon walked out a short way and signaled one of the several hacks ranged alongside the depot. "Take me to the Travelers Hotel, if it's still standin'."

"It was there this mornin' when I passed that way."

It paid to make sure, in a town that writhed with rapid growth and violent change. Concannon threw his valise

11

into the boxlike "station wagon" and climbed in beside it. "We can go the long way around," the driver said, "if you'd rather not travel along Bunco Alley."

Concannon was mildly flattered. The driver had taken him for gentility, or at least a well-to-do businessman. That was what came from working for a man like John Evers, who insisted that his agents dress and behave in a more or less civilized manner, especially if there was a possibility they would have to kill somebody. "Only gentlemen work for the railroad. And gentlemen are not murderers. Juries, anyhow, are not likely to believe they are, if they dress and look the part." That was the speech every new agent heard when he came to work for Evers, and then, if he cared about his job, he immediately went out and bought the best suit of clothes that he could pay for.

But Concannon proved to the driver that clothes did not always make the man. "Never mind takin' the long way around." He knew from experience that sooner or later he would find himself in that six-block section of saloons and gambling halls and dance halls and bordellos known, among other things, as Hell's Half Acre. The hack driver shrugged resignedly and turned onto that stretch of East Grand Avenue known as Bunco Alley.

Every town of any size had its Hell's Half Acre; Oklahoma City was no different from others in that respect. Concannon sat back in the hack and gazed indifferently at the blowsy prostitutes lounging in naked windows, the drunks, the pimps, the sharpshooters, and the gamblers.

The professional gunmen with .38-caliber bulges under their left arms, the knife specialists with the welted scars on the left side of their faces. The flashily dressed politicians, the almost invisible message carriers, the conveniently blind policemen, the silent, rib-shot mongrel dogs, as vicious as tigers. It was all a part of the Half Acre. They crossed Battle Row, where City Hall was crowded in between a swarm of saloons. Hop Boulevard, Maiden Lane.

From the black leather seat of the hack Concannon looked at it bleakly, listened to it, smelled it. He sighed faintly—it was almost like coming home. When you were a lawman, it was in places like the Half Acre that a man spent a great deal of his time, and, whatever the clothes he might be wearing, Concannon was a lawman.

The driver turned onto West Main and the atmosphere was immediately more respectable. The street had been recently scraped and was reasonably smooth. There were plank sidewalks here for the convenience of the better class of citizen, and wood awnings for his comfort. There were dress shops and jewelry stores, ice-cream parlors, and an opera house. Here was a new, quieter, more sedate world where rockaways and broughams mingled with the commoner buckboards and dray wagons.

Concannon came suddenly erect as the hack jolted past the North Robinson intersection. After a moment's hesitation, he called to the driver, "Pull up here. Take my grip on to the hotel."

He paid the hack driver and stepped up to the

plankwalk to where a small wooden sign swung forlornly in the wind: FINE AND DANDY CAFE. Through the plate-glass window he could see a man, heavy, balding, sweaty, leaning on the counter talking to a young woman. The *man* was obviously the cook, the woman the waitress. The counter ran almost the length of the small building and Concannon guessed that it would seat about fifteen diners. There were also three oilcloth-covered tables ranged along the plate-glass window. But it was the middle of the afternoon and there were no customers in the Fine and Dandy. Concannon opened the door and stepped inside.

The cook looked mildly irritated at the interruption, but he grinned pleasantly enough. "Too late for dinner and too early for supper, but I can cook you some eggs if you're hungry."

Concannon glanced at a glass pie case. "I'll just have a piece of that pie and some coffee."

"Apple or cherry? The apples come fresh from Arkansas."

"All right, the apple." Concannon sat at one of the tables by the window. Now that he was here, he wasn't sure what to do. What did you say to the widow of a man who had been your friend and had once saved your life? I'm sorry, ma'am, but my boss believes that your husband might have been a thief, and he's not real sure about you, either.

As the cook dished up the pie, Concannon looked at the waitress. Yes, he thought, he could see why Athena Allard had made an impression on John Evers. There

14

was something about her that was sensed rather than seen, a certain tension, like a spring that had been wound too tight. She was not an unusually small woman, but she was small boned which made her appear frail. Her hair was dark and lovely, her face small and almost childlike.

She put the coffee on the table and smiled, but only with her mouth. Then she brought the pie, and Concannon said, "Mrs. Allard, my name is Marcus Concannon. I was a friend of your husband when we were both riding for the court in Arkansas."

Instant hostility showed in her eyes. "What do you want? Are you from the newspapers?"

"No, ma'am. Like I said, Ray was my friend. I work for the railroad."

She relaxed a little, but not much. "There was a railroad man here before."

"My boss, John Evers. It's mostly because of him that I have to talk to you."

The cook, scowling angrily at Concannon, started around the end of the counter. But Athena shook her head impatiently, and he froze. She smiled faintly. "Don't mind Pat. He knows the trouble I've had with newspapermen; he just wants to protect me."

"Newspapermen?"

"The things they wrote about Ray." Her voice grew hard. "Saying he was a thief. That he was in with the robbers."

"I'm not a newspaperman, Mrs. Allard." Concannon took out his wallet and showed her his badge as a rail-

15

road detective. It was just a piece of nickel-plated metal with no real authority behind it, but there were people—politicians mostly—who viewed it with more respect than they would the star of a United States marshal. Athena Allard looked at it for a moment, then glanced at the cook. "It's all right, Pat." She sat down at the table and studied Concannon closely, as if she were quietly memorizing his commonplace features. "Yes," she said at last, "I remember your name. Ray liked to talk about the days—the good old days, he called them—when the two of you were deputy marshals riding for Parker."

Concannon didn't remember that period of starvation wages and sudden death at every turn as the "good old days," but he could understand that Ray Allard probably had. "Did Ray ever mention the time with the Pardu Bunch?"

Her thoughts seemed to turn inward. "Bob Pardu had you trapped in a gully. Ray shot him."

"There was more to it than that. I had been hurt, and my pistol was empty, and Bob Pardu had a shotgun in my face ready to shoot. I had already given Ray up for dead." For a moment he saw Ray lying there like a rag doll, in a spreading pool of his own blood. "But he wasn't dead, quite. He was alive enough to fire one more time and kill Pardu."

She did not seem very interested, and Concannon guessed that she had heard the story several times before. He said, "The reason I mention it is, Ray saved my life that day. I was his friend; I wouldn't do anything to hurt you."

"Not even if your boss told you to?"

"Not even then."

She smiled at him faintly. "I think I believe you, Mr. Concannon, but I don't want to be hurt any more. I don't want to talk about it."

"The trouble is," Concannon said uncomfortably, "a lot of people won't let it drop that easy. A hundred thousand dollars has been lost. If you don't talk to me, men from the railroad, or the express company, or the marshal's office, are sure to come to you with their questions. Some of those men will be even more unpleasant than I am."

"I don't understand why you come here now," she said wearily. "It's been more than a month since Ray was killed."

"I was up north at the time, on a job. Then my boss remembered that I was a pal of Ray's, so he wants me to go over the ground again and see if I can uncover something that maybe the others overlooked. John Evers is a very persistent man when a hundred thousand dollars is involved."

"All that money." A bitter smile touched her lips. "They don't care about Ray, just the money."

"That may be the case," Concannon told her, "with other people. But it's not the case with me . . . or you. You do want to see your husband's killer brought to justice, don't you?"

"Would that bring Ray back to life?"

"No, ma'am, but it would be some satisfaction . . ." He was putting it badly.

"Please go away," she said, not unkindly. "I'm sorry, I don't want to talk about it any more."

The big cook was sitting hunched over on the counter stool, watching them. Reluctantly, Concannon got to his feet. "I'm sorry, Mrs. Allard. I won't bother you any more, if I can help it." He paid for the pie and coffee and left the cafe. He crossed over to West Grand Avenue and walked the rest of the way to his hotel.

The Travelers was a two-story frame building which the management had faced with red brick in the hope it would look more substantial. It was still a reasonably respectable hotel, but newer and larger establishments were rapidly overtaking it. Within another year it would be torn down and something grander and more pretentious would go up in its place. Nothing remained the same for long in a town as new and volatile as Oklahoma City.

Concannon collected his grip from the clerk and climbed the stairs to his room. He went about unpacking and washing his face and shaving without actually noticing what the room was like. It might have been any of a thousand rooms in any middle-class hotel in Kansas City or Denver or Chicago. He had spent a good part of five years in such rooms, so alike that they were almost interchangeable.

He lathered his face in cold water from a blue china pitcher and cautiously began to shave. A long, undistinguished face looked back at him from the oak-framed mirror. The eyes were blue and direct, the mouth wide and not unpleasant. Marcus Concannon was not a complicated man; he enjoyed being a railroad detective, and he was good at it. He had been a lawman of one sort or another for most of his adult life—he and Ray Allard had been alike in that respect. He had never imagined himself as being anything different.

Being a lawman was, in some ways, like being a professional soldier. There were long periods of inactivity punctuated with brief bursts of violence. There were months on end that had to be given over to detail of the most boring sort; people to find, questions to ask, reports to write. But there were compensations in working for the railroad. The pay was good; he wore expensive worsted suits that he never could have afforded as a United States deputy marshal. Hack drivers mistook him for a well-to-do businessman.

Concannon grinned at himself in the mirror and finished shaving.

Then he found himself thinking about the robbery. Ray Allard had been a good lawman, with all the lawman's instincts for survival. It was difficult to think of Ray dead—he had had about him that special something that made him seem indestructible.

In spite of himself, Concannon found himself thinking, Was it more than just a simple robbery, after all, Ray? Did you get tired of living on a city marshal's pay? Did you go to the outlaws and make a deal with them to rob the company?

These were questions that had to be asked, and answers had to be found for them. Maybe he hadn't known Ray as well as he thought. Five years was a long time. Sudden responsibilities—marriage—could change a man. Even a man who had saved your life.

Nitroglycerin. If there was a key, that was it. Only experts and madmen worked with nitroglycerin, and madmen didn't bring off successful train robberies. "Sorry, Ray," Concannon said aloud to the face in the mirror. "I know you didn't take the money. That's what comes of working too long for a man like Evers."

He settled his shoulder holster and double-action .38 over his vest, then shrugged into his coat. Where would I go, he wondered, if I were an oilfield roustabout looking for a place to spend my share of that grass money.

He knew that answer only too well. The Half Acre.

CHAPTER 2

A three-piece Salvation Army band was playing at the corner of Broadway and Grand. Concannon dropped a quarter into the tambourine. The air smelled of wood-smoke and sour beer and rotting garbage and possibly some burning opium drifting in from the narrow alley known as Hop Boulevard. Down the street on South Broadway some loafers were urging on a dogfight. An angry whore on Alabaster Row screamed obscenities. Somewhere a wheel of fortune was clicking. Pickpockets moved like faded shadows through the small crowd that had gathered about the Army band.

Concannon strolled casually along Bunco Alley, toward the Santa Fe depot. Nothing that he saw or heard surprised or shocked him. It was all too familiar. In Leadville and Denver and end-of-track shanty towns— he had seen it all too many times before.

The Army's lady bass drum player sang aggressively. "How can a sinner know his sins on earth forgiven?" as the cornet player struggled to keep the pace. Concannon stopped in front of an establishment known as Lily's Day and Night. He sighed with a hint of resignation, for he had known from the beginning that he would wind up here. He always did.

Marvin Bone, sergeant of detectives, was sitting with his back to the far wall, idly studying a poker hand when Concannon entered the Day and Night. He acknowledged Concannon's presence with a sour look.

From behind the plank bar a strange bartender eyed Concannon suspiciously. A new banker was running the faro layout. New lamps hung over the gaming tables and the bare walls of the room had been freshly whitewashed. Even in a place like the Day and Night change was the order of the day.

Concannon stood for a moment taking it in. It was a small two-story frame building, almost identical to a dozen others like it on Bunco Alley. Two poker tables, the faro layout, seven-up, and a wheel of fortune. And the bar running half the length of the near wall. On the second floor there were living quarters for Lily Olsen, and individual rooms for the three house girls.

For almost four years Concannon had been returning to the Day and Night after a job in some distant place. It was almost like coming home. A poor home, some

21

would say—saloon-gambling hall-bordello—but it was the only one he had. Now, for the first time, it did not feel quite right to him. He sensed a certain chill. The girls lounging about the seven-up table looked harsh and unappealing.

Something, he thought quietly, is wrong here. But he knew instinctively that it was not the place, it was himself.

Detective Sergeant Marvin Bone was watching him with eyes as dark and quick as a hawk's. He was a heavy, colorless man in a plug hat and shapeless suit, and he sat uncomfortably on one buttock because of the awkward bulge of the .45 in his hip pocket. Suddenly the lawman threw in his hand, shoved himself up from the table and came toward Concannon.

"Did she tell you anything that she didn't tell the Oklahoma City police or the other railroad detectives?"

It took some time to get used to Bone's bluntness. Some people never did. "Marve," Concannon asked, "did you have somebody follow me when I got off the train today? I didn't know that I was that important."

"Anybody's important when there's a hundred thousand dollars involved."

"Ah." Concannon nodded knowingly. "The train robbery. But that was in the Chickasaw Nation, way out of your territory. Don't you have enough crime in Oklahoma City to keep you busy?"

The lawman smiled grimly. "One of these days I'll show you the inside of our cottonwood jail, Concannon. And throw away the key."

It was difficult to talk to Bone without having it end in a fight. Concannon sighed elaborately, then moved to the bar and signaled for whiskey. Bone followed him. "What did Allard's widow have to tell you today when you talked to her?"

Concannon idly watched the gamblers gathered around the faro layout. He asked mildly, "Didn't I hear somethin' about Oklahoma City passin' an anti-gamblin' ordinance?"

"Maybe," the lawman told him dryly. "But the council couldn't make up their mind just how 'anti' it ought to be. So they got together with the saloonkeepers and come to an understandin'. Once a month the police circulate amongst the saloons, and if they find any gamblin', the saloonkeeper is arrested and fined fifty dollars. That suits everybody fine, especially the police judges that collect the fines. I still want to know what Allard's widow told you."

"The same as she told you and all the others that have been talkin' to her. Nothin'."

"Does she know where that money is?"

"She didn't say."

"Concannon," Bone said coldly, "don't get fancy with me. You're just a railroad agent; that don't mean a thing here."

"That's queer. John Evers told me the chief of police would be glad to help me any way he could—all I had to do was ask."

"Don't believe ever'thing John Evers tells you—that's my advice."

The big policeman wheeled and tramped angrily out of the Day and Night. Well, Concannon thought to himself, he couldn't much blame Bone for being sour on the world. It wasn't easy being an honest policeman in a town that wasn't yet old enough to appreciate his worth.

The clatter of the wheel of fortune seemed to hesitate for just an instant. For one small part of a second every customer in the Day and Night seemed to stop talking at once. The lamps seemed to burn a little brighter and cleaner. Everybody sat back, a little more comfortable than they had been before. Nobody had to tell Concannon that Lily Olsen had entered the room.

Concannon turned and watched the mistress of the Day and Night making her smiling, joking, laughing way from the back of the saloon. She had Satan in her arms, stroking his silky, jet-black head. Smiling dazzlingly at one of the prosperous-looking poker players, she called, "Welcome to the Day and Night, Mr. Councilman . . . Bob," she shouted to the bartender, "bring another bottle over to the councilman's table. It's on the house, gentlemen."

She had not yet looked in Concannon's direction. "Howdy, Slim, I see your wife let you out tonight. Well, enjoy yourself while you can!" She waved to another customer halfway across the room. "Dolly's upstairs makin' herself pretty, Mr. Harkey. Any time you want to go up."

As if by accident she found herself at the bar standing next to Concannon. "Well," she said, stroking Satan's silky coat, "you took your time about comin' around."

"I had some things to see about first." Like everybody else in the saloon, he was warmed by her presence. "It's good to be back, Lily. As always."

"Well," she said dryly, "you can sit down now and buy me a drink, and tell me about all the men you've whipped and the women you've loved since you've been gone."

The new bartender knew what to do; he quickly cleared the customers from a table at the end of the bar and set up two glasses and a bottle of Tennessee whiskey. Concannon filled the glasses. They saluted and downed the nut-brown bourbon. Satan sat on the table and looked at Concannon coolly with sun-yellow eyes. After a moment Lily said, "I'm sorry about Ray."

For an instant Concannon could almost see Ray sitting there, boyishly handsome, laughing. It was still hard to think of him dead. "Well," he heard himself saying, "it wasn't like he was a green hand. He knew the chances that went with the job."

"Is that the reason you came back to Oklahoma City? Because of Ray."

"I came back to Oklahoma City because this is where John Evers wanted me." He reached across the table and scratched Satan's ear. Satan was a coal-black alley cat who lived like a maharajah in the Day and Night. His coat shone like Mandarin silk. He had dined that night on fresh New Orleans oysters, more rare than gold coin, and the red flesh of an exotic fish from cold, far-off waters. That repast had been washed down with heavy cream and the nose-tickling froth of St. Louis beer.

Mister, Concannon thought to himself, if you don't come down with the gout there is no justice in the world.

He sat back and looked at the cat's mistress. They were two of a kind in many ways—strong, well cared for, sleek and handsome. Lily smiled. "Are you goin' to find that money?"

"A month after the robbery? You don't think it would still be in Oklahoma Territory, do you?"

"Why did Evers bring you here then?"

It was strange how the thought of a hundred thousand dollars fascinated people. Railroad executives, bordello keepers, police detectives—sooner or later the subject always came around to that money. "There would be a bonus in it for you, wouldn't there?" Lily asked casually. "If you did find it?"

"I don't count on finding it. Anybody smart enough to rob the Santa Fe is smart enough to get out of the country with the money. All the same . . ." He shrugged defensively. "Lily, are there any oilfield workers in town? Well shooters, explosive haulers, anybody like that?"

"Ah!" She grinned. "The nitroglycerin. I wondered if anybody would ever get around to lookin' into that." She poured another round of Tennessee whiskey. "There was somebody in here yesterday, lookin' for a man to take a nitro wagon down to the Choctaw Nation. Last I heard he was askin' around the honkytonks on Hop Boulevard."

Concannon downed his whiskey. "Thanks, Lily. I'll see if I can find him."

"Will I see you later?"

26

He hesitated—only for an instant, but Lily noticed. "Later," he said. "Just as always."

Hop Boulevard was the end of the line for men who had been going down for a long time. Here a man might be murdered for the gold in his teeth or a glass setting in a ring—many had been murdered for less. One-room honkytonks, twelve-by-twelve cribs and scrap lumber shacks lined the cluttered alley. Next to the Santa Fe tracks Concannon found the dirty canvas tent known as the Paris Cafe.

It was still a little early for places like the Paris. "I'm lookin' for a man that's been askin' for nitro haulers," Concannon said to the bartender.

The bartender eyed Concannon's expensive suit and instinctively reached for a bung starter beneath the bar. One of the cafe's two customers, a leathery, steely-eyed man in laceup boots and a wolf skin coat, moved along the bar toward Concannon. "I'm Sam Speer. You don't look like no nitro hauler to me."

"I'm not. But I'd like to talk to you, if you've got the time."

Speer shrugged indifferently. "Sooner or later a drunk will come in here and decide that life ain't worth livin' no more, then I'll convince him that he'd be doin' hisself a favor to drive my nitro wagon down to the Choctaw Nation. If he blows hisself up, what's the difference? If he don't, why maybe he'll make enough on the job to get hisself straightened out." He grinned sourly. "But that won't happen for some time yet. Two, three hours after midnight, that's when the drunks get to feelin' low, and that's when I'll get my man" He sized up Concannon with a practiced eye. "If you've got the money for whiskey, I've got the time for talk."

Concannon paid for a bottle and took it to a table. The label on the bottle said, *Kentucky Bourbon. Four years old. Aged in oak barrels.* Concannon knew that it was raw alcohol liberally spiced with red pepper and colored with tobacco. Trade whiskey, they called it. A barrel of it could kill more Indians than a regiment of heavy cavalry.

Concannon poured himself a drink to be sociable but did not taste it. "How many well shooters," he asked casually, "would you say are in the Territory?"

Speer downed his poisoned alcohol without blinking an eye. "That depends. Are you talkin' about men that know their jobs, men that can lower a shot into a hole and bring in a well without gettin' theirselves blowed up? Or men like I have to settle for most of the time, the drunks and the simple minded."

"Men who know everything there is to know about explosives."

The oilman shrugged. "You can count them on one hand. Al Galley—but he's off in Pennsylvania somewheres, wildcattin'. There's Jack Sewell and Weeb Carter, up in the Cherokee country. And Charlie Buckwhite, he's sniffin' around the Creek Nation, lookin' to make a big strike. That's all there is." He thought for a moment and then said, "There's Ab Miller, the best of the pack, but I don't know where he is now."

Concannon sat a little straighter. "What do you mean?"

28

"Don't know where he's at, that's all. Maybe a month, six weeks ago, I tried to get him to do a job for me. But he said he was busy. Had a job with somebody else."

"Did he say who?"

"Maybe he did. But I don't recollect." Speer helped himself to another drink of the Paris Cafe's whiskey.

"Where were you when you talked to Miller?"

"Here in Oklahoma City. I was here contractin' for cable tools and ran into him on Broadway. The stretch they call Battle Row."

"Have you got any notion how I could get in touch with him now?"

Speer shook his head. "No tellin' about well shooters. They go whichever way the wind blows. There's one thing about Ab, though. Wherever he's at, he's drawin' top pay."

"Because he's the best?"

"That, too. But mostly because Ab's got a powerful likin' for money. No harm in that, of course."

"Where would the best payin' jobs likely be right now?"

Speer sipped his liquid poison as if it were fine brandy. "That's somethin' of a puzzle. There ain't no big play in oil here in the Territory—not yet, anyhow. A few shallow wells up in the Cherokee Nation. Some wildcattin' down amongst the Choctaws. But nothin' that would attract a man like Ab. Maybe he's up amongst the Creeks lookin' for that big strike that'll make him rich."

"Has he got a wife, or maybe some friends that would know where to find him?"

"Wife? Ab?" The oilman chuckled. He picked up the whiskey bottle and admired it for a moment. "Wait a minute," he said. "There's Maggie Slatter. Seems like her and Ab was keepin' company once. She might know where to find him."

"Where would I find Maggie Slatter?"

The oilman shrugged his shoulders. "If it was me lookin' for her, I'd try one of the houses on West Second Street."

The area west of the Frisco freight house, on Second Street, served one useful purpose—by comparison it made the Half Acre section seem sedate and well mannered. Concannon picked his way fastidiously through the rubble and rubbish that clogged the rutted street. Somewhere in the night a woman screamed. A man reeled out of one of the houses, stumbled a few feet and fell on his face across the dirt walk. Casually, a woman followed him out of the house, turned him over with her foot and expertly rifled his pockets.

She looked up as Concannon approached, dropped the man's gold watch into the bosom of her dress and grinned. "Lookin' for a good time, honey? You can't do no better'n Madame McDonnald's." She jerked her head toward the house that she had just come out of.

The man on the ground groaned and struggled to roll over on his stomach. "I'm lookin' for Maggie Slatter," Concannon said. The man on the ground grasped one of Concannon's legs and tried to pull himself to his feet. His head was bleeding and, in the light from Madame

McDonnald's open doorway, his eyes looked glassy and wild. Concannon shook him off and moved out of his reach.

"Maggie Slatter!" The woman peered at him sharply, her mouth turned down. "Honey, you sure don't look like *her* type. But I guess it takes all kinds." She brushed off her hands and started up the walk to the house. Her victim on the ground had finally hauled himself to his hands and knees and was slowly crawling off toward a redbud bush at the corner of Madame McDonnald's front yard.

Concannon took a greenback out of his pocket. "It's worth somethin' to me to find Maggie Slatter."

The woman turned, looked sharply at the greenback. "Well," she said, snapping up the bill and stuffing it into her bosom with the watch, "you won't find her in none of the *decent* houses, I can tell you that much. Try the cribs on the other side of the street."

For some time Concannon stood on the corner of Second and North Walker. The customer from Madame McDonnald's had made it as far as the redbud bush and was now ridding himself of the tincture of opium that someone had put in his drink. A steady stream of passenger hacks were letting out customers in front of Noah's Ark, Nina Truelove's, and, on the next corner, the famous house of "Creole" girls. What I need, Concannon thought grimly, is a drink. But he didn't dare risk it in any of the places on Second Street.

He crossed the street and took a dirt path behind Noah's Ark, where the cribs were. The tiny boxboard shacks, just big enough to hold a bed and a washstand, leaned wearily against each other in the alley. Pimps hissed at him from the darkness. Women, some of them in sleazy pink slips, some not, called to him from open doorways. Somewhere in the night dice were rattling. A woman laughed. A man cursed savagely. A dog began to howl.

A pimp sidled along the back porch of Noah's Ark and called softly, "Creole girls, mister? Want to change your luck?"

Concannon decided that he'd rather deal with the pimp than canvas the area crib by crib. He gestured the man out of the shadows. "Maggie Slatter. You know her?"

"Four bits," the pimp said quickly.

Concannon dug out two quarters and handed them over. The pimp darted along the path and Concannon followed. Some of the women hooted at them, some of them made obscene gestures and laughed. Most of them merely sat in their open doorways, harshly backlighted by coal-oil lamps, and stared blankly. "There it is," the pimp said at last, pointing. "The crib next to the one on the end." He shrugged his bony shoulders and looked disappointed. From a man of Concannon's appearance he had expected something better.

Concannon moved forward. "Maggie Slatter?"

The woman slouched forward on a canebottom chair, her slight, bony figure edged in the reddish light of her lamp. Concannon couldn't see much of her face until she turned to look at him. A great red scar streaked down her left cheek from her hairline to her chin. Her mouth on that side pulled up in a permanent obscene grin, and her left eye was white and sightless.

"What do you want?" she asked.

"Talk. About Ab Miller. I'm willin' to pay."

She stared at him with her one good eye. "How much?" The question was filled with weariness and little hope. The hideously scarred whore in the next to the end crib on Second Street—what would her normal price be? Fifty cents? A dollar at most. Recklessly, Concannon said, "Five dollars. If you can help me."

The scarred side of her face showed nothing. The uninjured side looked stunned. She stood up. "Come in."

There was little room for two people to maneuver inside the crib. Maggie Slatter quickly closed the door and shoved the chair in between the bed and the wall. Concannon sat gingerly on the edge of the chair; Maggie sat at the foot of the bed. She wore the Second Street whore's uniform, the soiled pink slip, but she did not seem to notice that she was almost naked, and after a moment neither did Concannon.

"Do you know where Ab Miller is?" Concannon asked.

Sadly, she shook her head. "He's been gone more'n a month. Five, six weeks, maybe. I don't know where he went."

Concannon took a greenback out of his pocket and handed it to her. "Didn't Ab say anything when he left to give you a notion where he might be headed?"

She looked at the greenback with her good eye, holding the bill in both hands as if it were a baby. "Ab never said he was goin' anywheres at all. One day he just left." She smiled with the uninjured side of her face. "I figgered he just got tired of me."

"Did Ab have any friends that might know where to find him?"

"Ab never had many friends. He was a loner."

"Business friends, maybe?"

She thought for a minute and then shook her head. "I don't recollect any. I ain't bein' much help, am I?"

"Did Ab ever talk to you about his business. The oil business?"

The question seemed to surprise her. "Not much, but sometimes. At nights mostly. He would wake up in a sweat, sick and shakin', like he was full of poison whiskey."

"Do you know what was wrong with him?"

"He was scared," she said matter of factly. "Who wouldn't be? Like to get hisself blowed up any minute. I guess he dreamed about it." She got a faraway look. "One night when he woke up like that he said to me, 'Maggie, I ain't goin' to stay in this business much longer. I got plans for us. We're goin' to move away from here, me and you. We'll go somewheres and settle down and live like anybody else.' I thought he meant it." The blind eye looked at Concannon. "Wasn't that a fool thing for me to do?"

"I don't know. Maybe he did mean it. When did this happen?"

Maggie made an ineffectual gesture with one hand. "Just before he went off and never came back. I should of known he didn't mean it."

The scarred side of her face was as expressionless as a stone mask. Somehow that made it even more appealing when a single tear welled up in her good eye and slid almost unseen down her smooth right cheek. Concannon turned his head while she fumbled for a handkerchief.

For the first time Concannon noticed that the crib, in an effort to keep out the summer dust and the winter wind, had been papered with old newspapers. He read the headlines from a four-year-old *Ford County Globe*: WAR IN OKLAHOMA. SOONERS AND ARMY IN PITCHED BATTLE.

In the back of his mind he was thinking something else. Ab Miller, an expert with nitroglycerin, had been running a case of nerves and wanted out of the business. He and Maggie Slatter (so he had said) had planned to leave the territory. According to Sam Speer, Miller had also been a man who liked money. Most important of all, Miller had been missing ever since the train robbery and hadn't been heard from since. Ab Miller was sounding more and more like a man that Concannon would like very much to talk to.

He stood up in the cramped space between the wall and the bed. "Much oblige for talkin' to me, Maggie. If you think of a way I might find Ab, will you get in touch with me at the Travelers Hotel?"

She nodded distractedly and dabbed at her good eye. "Maggie," he asked quietly, "do you recollect that Ab Miller ever mentioned a man by the name of Ray Allard?"

She shook her head slowly.

"A lawman, used to be. He was ridin' shotgun for special shipments on the Santa Fe." The question left a bitterness in his mouth. He thought: Sorry, Ray, but I've got to be sure.

Maggie looked at Concannon and sighed. "No, I don't recollect anybody called Allard."

"When Miller was talkin' about movin' you away from here and settlin' down. Did he say how he was goin' to get the money for that?"

"Money?" The uninjured side of her face stiffened. "I guess I never thought about it. What does it matter? He never meant it."

Concannon reached for the door. "Good night, Maggie. If you think of anything, I'll be at the Travelers."

He caught a hack that had just let out a customer at Nina Truelove's. "Take me to Lily Olsen's." The hack jolted across the Frisco tracks and turned east on Main. Within a matter of minutes they were back in the raucous, violent atmosphere of Battle Row. A group of drunk cowhands staggered across the street in front of City Hall. One of them fired his pistol in the air and almost started a dozen runaways. But Concannon settled back in the hack and waited patiently for the commotion to settle—after the grim, dark violence of West Second Street this seemed like good clean fun.

The hack stopped in front of the Day and Night and Concannon got out. Detective Sergeant Marvin Bone was standing spread-legged in front of the establishment, his hands clasped rigidly behind his back, as if he had been waiting there especially for Concannon's return.

Concannon decided that for once he would get ahead of Bone in the policeman's favorite question and answer game. "Bone," he asked quickly, as soon as he was out of the hack, "what do you know about an oil well shooter by the name of Ab Miller?"

The detective looked at him with displeasure. "What makes you want to know?"

"It strikes me that Miller might have had a hand in stealin' that grass money. He's an expert with explosives, he wanted money, and he disappeared about the time the train was robbed."

Bone's sour expression did not change. "And he lived a while with a Second Street whore. Is that all Maggie Slatter could tell you?"

Concannon grinned. He would have been disappointed if Bone hadn't already looked into the disappearance of Miller. "Come in the Day and Night. I'll buy you a drink."

Bone spat at the ground, hitched his pants that were sagging under the weight of his .45 and walked away. Concannon drew a cigar wallet from his inside pocket, selected a straight, dark wrapper corona and lit it with pleasure. It was not as good as John Evers' excellent green wrapper Cubans, but good enough for an ordinary railroad detective. He started up the steps to Lily's saloon.

Somebody hissed at him from the far side of the Day and Night. A lanky gray figure was crouching back in the shadows. "Mister, you lookin' for Ab Miller?"

The voice was familiar. It had been trying to sell him a Creole girl the last time Concannon had heard it. He left the steps and moved cautiously toward the shadowy figure of the pimp. "What do you know about Miller?"

"I heard you talkin' to Maggie. Maybe I can tell you where to find him, if the price is right." He shot nervous glances up and down Bunco Alley. "Come around here out of the light. I don't want to be seen talkin' to a railroad detective."

Concannon stepped quickly into the deep shadows alongside the Day and Night. At the last moment—when it was much too late to do anything about it—he realized that it was an extremely foolish thing to do. An object cold and hard, which could only have been a pistol barrel, swished in the darkness. The pimp stepped back, grinning widely, his hands held out in front of him as proof of his own innocence in the matter.

Concannon didn't see it. There was a fire in his brain. He started to fall and a pair of strong hands grabbed him and hauled him into the narrow alleyway between the Day and Night and the next honkytonk. A fist exploded against his ribs. Concannon gasped and fell to his knees. Two men began kicking him with heavy brogans in a way that was both impersonal and deadly. The pimp stood a short distance away, grinning delightedly.

Then, unexpectedly, the kicking stopped. One of the men hunkered down beside Concannon and said quietly, "That was just a friendly warnin', Concannon. Stop botherin' folks about Ab Miller and other things that

38

ain't none of your business." Big, strong hands took Concannon's shoulders and shook him. "You hear me, mister?"

Concannon worked his mouth but could make no sound. The pimp giggled. One of the kickers shrugged indifferently and spat at the wall of the Day and Night. "He hears."

"Is that right?" the second brogan wearer asked. "Do you hear me, Concannon?"

Concannon groaned. ". . . Yes."

"Who was it told you to start askin' questions about Miller?"

Concannon breathed in and out very carefully. One of the men, reading his mind, neatly snatched his .38 from his shoulder holster and flipped it away. "Don't get fancy, Concannon. We don't want to kill you. Now who was it put you to lookin' for Ab Miller?"

". . . Nobody," Concannon managed with some difficulty. "It seemed like the obvious thing to do. A safe was blown open with nitroglycerin. So I look for a nitroglycerin expert."

"Obvious, maybe," one of the men said dryly, "but not healthy. Do you know what you're goin' to do now?"

Concannon made a vague sound. "What you're goin' to do," the man continued, "is nothin'. You're goin' to forget about Ab Miller and nitroglycerin and all the rest of it. You're goin' to tell your boss the trail's too cold to follow." He paused to allow his lecture to sink in. "You do like we tell you, Concannon, and we won't have to come back and kill you."

CHAPTER 3

The next voice Concannon heard was that of Detective Sergeant Marvin Bone. "Come alive, Concannon. I got better things to do than wet-nurse railroad agents."

Concannon entered the world of reality with great reluctance. His head throbbed. His ribs felt as if they were splintered. He lay on his back staring up at a group of mildly curious faces, although it was nothing unusual to find a man beaten to unconsciousness in Bunco Alley. He saw that someone had dragged him out of the narrow space between the two honkytonks to a lighted area in front of the Day and Night. ". . . How long have I been here?"

Bone shrugged. "Two, three minutes since I heard *you* carryin' on and dragged you out to the light. You want to tell me who done it?"

"What would you do, give them a reward?"

The policeman grinned. The onlookers began to get bored and most of them drifted away. "You figger you're able to walk?" the policeman asked.

Concannon groaned resignedly. Sooner or later it had to be faced. With Bone's help, he pulled himself to his knees, then to his feet. When he began to sway, Bone sat him on the steps to the Day and Night. "Here," the policeman said acidly, handing Concannon his double-action .38. "This was in the alley where I found you. I don't know why you bother to carry it."

Concannon held his head. He had given a shameful

40

performance, and nobody knew it better than himself, but he felt too miserable to worry about it now. The rest of the onlookers drifted away and for a moment Bone and Concannon were left to themselves. "How many was there?" Bone asked.

"Two. And a Second Street pimp." He told the detective everything he knew, which was almost nothing.

"You think one of your heavy-footed pals was Ab Miller?"

Concannon thought about it. "No. I don't know why, but I don't think so."

"Do you figger they was part of the bunch that robbed the train?"

Concannon had already done some thinking about that. "Why would the outlaws stay so close to the scene of the robbery when they could just as easily move on to a safer part of the country?"

"I was hopin' you'd be able to explain that to me."

Concannon grinned weakly. He noticed that his nose was dripping blood down the front of his vest. "Bone, I've had a hard night. I've been fed poisoned whiskey in the Paris Cafe, I spent an hour in a Second Street crib talkin' to a mutilated whore, and I've been bushwhacked. Do I have to go on listenin' to questions that I don't know the answers to?"

The policeman showed his teeth in a wolfish grin. "All right, Ill talk to you tomorrow, if you manage to stay alive that long."

As Bone strolled away toward Battle Row, Lily Olsen, with Satan in one arm, flew down the steps of the Day and Night. Appalled, she stared at Concannon. "What *happened* to you?"

Concannon sighed, a world of weariness in the sound. "Lily, it's a long story and I don't think I'm up to talkin' about it right now."

Lily put Satan down and looked closely at Concannon. "Is your nose broken?"

"It's not my nose that I'm worried about. Do you mind if I go up to your place and clean up a little and take stock?"

The mistress of the Day and Night gestured impatiently, then grabbed up the cat in one arm and helped Concannon with the other. The saloon's customers watched with elaborate indifference as Concannon limped the length of the long room and made his way slowly up to the second floor. "Sit down," Lily told him, opening the door to her living quarters. "There's liquor by the washstand. I'll get Bob to heat some water."

Lily disappeared, and Concannon headed for the bottle of whiskey. He winced as he looked at himself in the diamond-dust mirror above Lily's dresser. The whiskey warmed his insides and eased his aching ribs, but it did not make his battered face any less battered or his filthy clothes any cleaner. He sagged onto the crocheted coverlet of Lily's bed and swigged from the neck of the bottle.

Satan sat on the floor and looked up at him with polite indifference. For the moment Concannon was too tired to think about his recent adventure; he merely sat, his mind blank, taking frequent drinks of Lily's excellent

Tennessee whiskey. It had been a long while since he had seen the inside of Lily's living quarters, but it hadn't changed much, except to grow slightly more lavish. The walls were covered with dark brown and red velvet—a foot of the wall, Concannon thought, would cost as much as a middling suit of clothes. The huge gilt-framed mirror over her dresser glittered with diamond dust, like the mirrors in the Windsor Hotel in Denver. The furniture was both heavy and graceful, and elaborately carved. A large lamp glowed softly at one end of the dresser, its shade a jungle of hand-painted roses.

All in all it was exactly the sort of room that a prosperous madam on Bunco Alley would choose for herself. Concannon liked it.

Satan pounced onto a needlepoint chair and went to sleep. Concannon had disposed of almost half of the whiskey when Lily returned with a large china bowl of hot water. There was a certain cheerful professionalism in the way she briskly arranged her equipment and went to work. She took the bottle out of his hand, unbuttoned his shirt, and in a moment had him neatly stripped to the waist.

She lathered a cloth with lilac-scented soap and went to work. "You're goin' to be stove up for a day or so, but I don't think any ribs are broken. Do you want me to send for a doc?"

"No. All I need now is some rest and some time to think."

"I hope you don't aim to go lookin' for the toughs that did this to you."

Concannon made a weary sound. "Believe me, that's the last thought in my mind." Expertly, Lily cleaned his face of blood and filth. She dabbed the cuts and bruises with a mixture of turpentine and whiskey. "Have you ever given any thought," she said dryly, running her fingers over a variety of old gunshot wounds and knife scars, "to goin' into another line of business?"

Concannon made a meaningless sound and lay back on the bed. Lily said casually, "We could get married, you know. Run the Day and Night together. It would be better than gettin' yourself beat half to death in a dark alley."

They had been over this ground several times before and Concannon still wasn't sure if she meant it. He watched her thoughtfully as she expertly sponged his battered torso. Lily was like the room she lived in; Concannon liked her and was comfortable with her. Whether there was more to it than that, he didn't know.

"Sit up," she told him. Wincing, Concannon shoved himself erect and sat perfectly still while Lily rubbed him down with liniment and bound him with strips of white sheeting. When she was through, she stood back and looked at her work thoughtfully. "That'll hold your ribs in place for a while, but you'd better see a regular doc."

"You're all the doc I need, Lily." Maybe she was right. Maybe he would be smart to marry a Bunco Alley madam and save himself a lot of pain. At the moment, with Lily standing there in the soft light of the rose-colored lamp, it didn't seem like a bad idea.

She handed him the bottle and he took a drink. "Concannon," she said softly, shaking her head from side to side, "lay down"

Concannon did as she ordered. She took off his shoes, then she unbuttoned his pants and took them off. He lay on the bed in his underdrawers, bone tired and half drunk. More from habit than for any other reason, he reached for her.

She slapped his hand away. "Plenty of time for that when you're not stove up. Get some sleep now."

". . . Lily."

She looked down at him. "Yes?"

"My first day back in Oklahoma City, I didn't aim for it to work out just the way it has. But anyway, it's good to be back."

She smiled faintly. "Go to sleep, Concannon."

She turned down the wick and blew out the lamp.

Concannon lay for a while in the darkness. Lord, he thought, I feel a hundred years old! It seemed that he could feel every injury that he had ever received. All his hard days in the saddle, all the sleepless nights, weighed down on him. Just before he fell asleep, the face of Athena Allard flashed in his mind for some unexplainable reason. And he felt even older than before.

Once during the night he came awake with a start and there was something warm and furry pressed against him. It was Satan. Well, he thought, I guess a cat is better company than no company at all. In the vague distance he could hear the sound of a raw, new town winding up the night. Somewhere the last gambler was losing his

45

last dollar at faro. The last drunk was beginning to fall. The policeman in Bunco Alley was taking his last turn of the street.

The Day and Night was silent.

The next time Concannon came awake it was with a slant of dazzling sunlight on his face. "Here," Lily said, skillfully filling a cup with black coffee and hot milk from twin pots. It was a habit that she had picked up on Bourbon Street in New Orleans and brought with her to Oklahoma. "Drink this."

Cautiously, Concannon shoved himself up in bed and drank the pale, hot coffee. His head ached. His face was sore and discolored, and his ribs were still tender. But at that, he felt considerably better than he had the night before.

Lily gave him a few minutes to take stock of himself, then she said, "You've got company. Marvin Bone's downstairs wantin' you to testify at a coroner's inquest."

He looked at her blankly. "Who's dead?"

"Bone didn't say."

"What time is it?"

"Ten o'clock. Bone wants you at the undertaker's by eleven."

"What Bone wants,". Concannon said wearily, "Bone usually gets. One way or another." He moved the still sleeping cat out of the way and swung his bare feet to the floor. Lily gave him his suit on a hanger; it had been sponged and brushed and looked reasonably presentable. Concannon began to get himself dressed.

Bone was sitting at the seven-up table looking even more sour than usual when Concannon came down.

"What's this about a coroner's inquest?"

"It's the way we do things now," the policeman told him snappishly. "Somebody gets hisself killed, there's an inquest. Keeps us busy. Ain't everybody can lay in bed till the middle of the day."

"Who got himself killed that I could testify about?"

"That's what I want you to tell me when you see the body."

They left the Day and Night and walked toward Broadway. Within a few minutes Concannon was gasping for breath; Lily's bandaging had kept his ribs in place all right, but it didn't leave much room for breathing. "Bone, whereabouts have you got this body that you want me to look at?"

"At the undertaker's on Harvey."

"And how do you expect to get to that place?"

Bone shot him a pitying look. "Walk, of course. Or did you think the city would outfit us with a spring rig and a pair of high-steppin' bays?"

Concannon pulled up panting and flagged a passing hack. "We'll ride, if it's all the same to you."

There was early autumn in the air, a taste of dust and steel. They rode in silence, with Bone shifting one way and the other because of the bulky .45 in his hip pocket. "Pull up here," the policeman said at last, as the driver turned off Main onto Harvey.

The undertaker's was a small frame house sitting in a weed patch well back from the street. A sign in front announced in new paint: FUNERALS. GRAVEDIGGING. TOMBSTONES CUT TO ORDER. Bone and Concannon went up a dirt path to where the coroner was waiting for them on the front porch.

"This here's Doc Mayhew," Bone said shortly, by way of introduction. "You got the customer ready to look at, Doc?"

The doctor, a gray, tired-looking man, nodded to Concannon. "Ready as he'll ever be, I guess." He led the way through the house to where the body was laid out in the back room. The undertaker, a large nervous man by the name of Lawson, was looking down at his handiwork and shaking his head sadly. "No money, no folks. Nothin'. The city ought to know that a body can't get a decent burial without money. The council don't stop to think about things like that."

Bone looked at Concannon. "How about it? Do you recognize him?"

The dead man had been small and pallid. His face had a tense, pinched look, even in death. His eyes were blue, washed out, and now they looked faraway and vaguely thoughtful. "He's the pimp that I saw last night on Second Street," Concannon said. "And after that he was at the Day and Night. Him and his two pals that took turns kickin' me."

The doctor was writing in a notebook. The undertaker was still shaking his head. "You know his name," Doc Mayhew asked.

"No. Most likely some of the crib girls would know. He's the one that took me to Maggie Slatter."

The doctor blinked. This last statement of Concannon's made no sense to him, but he let it go. "By rights," he said, "I guess there ought to be somebody here to swear you in before hearin' your testimony. But I can't see that it makes much difference." He looked questioningly at the policeman, and Bone shrugged. "Is that all you know about him?"

"That's all. Just the two times is all I saw of him."

The doctor drew a sheet over the body and Concannon and Bone went back to the porch. "How did he die?" Concannon asked.

"Stabbed in the back. Not very neat, but it did the work."

They walked down the path to Harvey. "Where did it happen?"

"In the alley, not far from where I found you. Looks like the other two didn't want any witnesses to the beating. Hard luck for the pimp." They stood by the side of the dirt street, looking off toward the main part of town. "Is any of this," Bone asked dryly, "beginnin' to give you any ideas?"

"A couple. The pimp must have heard me askin' Maggie about Ab Miller. He took his story to somebody he figgered would be interested. They caught me in front of the Day and Night, and we know the rest."

Bone pulled his mouth down to show that he didn't like it. "Why didn't they kill you instead of just knockin' you around some?"

"A good question, but I don't know the answer."

"Queer," Bone said in a thoughtful tone, "that they'd

49

walk off and leave the job half done. Maybe it was a mistake. Maybe they thought you was dead. Maybe when they find out different they'll come back and do this job right. Have you thought about that?"

"It crossed my mind. Now if you're through with me, I think I'll go to the hotel and get a change of clothes."

There was a message waiting for Concannon when he got to the Travelers. *Mr. Concannon, I would like to talk to you. Tonight after supper, if it is convenient. I'll wait at the cafe.* It was signed, *Athena Allard.*

"Who brought this?" Concannon asked the clerk.

"A man. About your age, I guess, heavy-set, not much hair."

That would be Pat Duncan, owner and chief cook of the Fine and Dandy Cafe. "Did he say anything?"

"Just to give you this message."

Concannon went to his room and sat for some time thinking about Athena Allard. He was ridiculously pleased that she had asked to see him, although he knew that it was nothing personal.

He shaved and changed clothes, then he went down to the lobby and spent the best part of the afternoon writing letters to all the lawmen he knew who might be able to tell him something about an oil well shooter by the name of Ab Miller. For John Evers he wrote a brief report, sketching the highlights of his recent adventures without going into great detail. He read the report to himself and didn't like it. "Bumbling" and "inept" were two words that occurred to him as he put the report in an envelope and sealed it. He was sure the same words would also occur to Evers.

As he was about to leave the hotel a uniformed policeman came in and asked the clerk for Marcus Concannon. Concannon sighed resignedly and gave himself up.

"It's Sergeant Bone," the patrolman said. "He wants to talk to you."

"Did he say what about?"

"No, sir. He's over on West Second Street in one of the—ah—places of business there. He said you'd know where to come."

Concannon had a sinking feeling in his gut. "All right. Are you comin' along too?"

"Yes, sir. Sergeant Bone said to escort you."

"I don't guess he sent a rig of some kind, did he, so that we wouldn't have to walk?"

The idea of riding seemed to startle the lawman. "No, sir, he sure never did anything like that."

They went outside and Concannon stopped a passing hack.

Bone was waiting for them outside Maggie Slatter's crib. Doc Mayhew and a uniformed policeman brought a covered body out of the shack and were loading it into the undertaker's black hearse.

"It was a big day for the undertaker when you landed in Oklahoma City," Bone told Concannon sourly. "Everybody you come in contact with winds up dead. You're worse'n Typhoid Mary."

Concannon glanced at the body in the hearse. "Maggie

Elizabeth Slatter—goin' by what it says on a marriage certificate that we found in her shack," the sergeant continued. "Did you know she was married?"

"No."

"Me neither until I got to talkin' to some of the other girls. Henry Slatter, corn whiskey drinker and wife beater. Henry got hisself lickered up three years ago and fell under a dray wagon and was killed. Maggie's been here ever since"

It was an ugly story but no uglier than many others that Concannon knew about. "How did she die?"

"Stabbed in the back with a big blade. Does that remind you of somethin'?"

"The pimp."

The sergeant smiled. "Maggie was stiff as a board when one of the girls found her and sent for us. The doc figgers she was killed last night sometime. About the time you was gettin' kicked in the alley alongside the Day and Night, maybe."

"Did the pimp do it?"

"The girls say no, and I take their word for it."

"My two pals in the alley, then?"

"Unless you've got enemies that we don't know about."

"Are you doin' anything to find them?"

Bone flashed a savage grin. "We're thinkin' about it. Come in the shack, I want to show you somethin'."

The two men crowded into the tiny crib. A trunk had been opened and systematically rifled. A plush-bound "memory book" lay opened on the bed. Bone picked up the book and showed Concannon a stamp-sized tintype picture. The man in the picture appeared to be in his early thirties, strong, big boned, rugged.

"Ab Miller," the policeman said with pleasure. "Do you recognize him?"

"No."

"He was a pal of Ray Allard's. Did the explosive work in the robbery. And you was a pal of Allard's too."

"Does that make me one of the outlaws?"

Bone shrugged. "Maybe not, but it stands to reason that you would know some of Allard's pals."

"It hasn't been proved that Ray and Miller even knew each other."

The sergeant chuckled to himself. "Proof. A mighty handy thing, when you don't have it."

Striving for a casual tone, Concannon asked, "Could I take that picture for a few hours? I'll give you a receipt."

Bone looked at him sharply. "Why?"

"I don't know. But the minute I started asking about Miller two people get killed and I get a fine collection of bruises. I'd like to get to know him better."

Surprisingly, the policeman lifted the tintype out of the book and handed it over. "Oh yes," Bone said, gazing innocently at the ceiling, "there's one more thing we found. I guess it's what the killer was lookin' for when he tore up the place. But we found it under the floor where Maggie had put it." From his pocket he took out a bundle of crisp new greenbacks.

Concannon took the packet and quickly counted it. The bills were all twenties, there were twenty-five of them. He whistled under his breath. "Five hundred dollars."

"Brand new," Bone said comfortably. "Does that make you think of anything?"

"I know," Concannon sighed, "you think it's from the grass money shipment. Do you have any proof?"

"No, but it's a right interestin' thing to think about. Ab Miller knew that Maggie was on to his robbery scheme. First he tried to buy her off with the five hundred dollars—but then they got wind that she was talkin' to a railroad agent, so they decided to play it safe and make sure that she didn't talk any more."

"I hate to keep bringin' it up, that it's still all guesswork. You don't have any proof."

Bone flashed his unpleasant grin. "About all these killin's that started happenin' the minute you landed in Oklahoma City. They make me look bad, and I don't like that."

Concannon felt as if someone had just placed a heavy load on his shoulders—he knew that Bone was about to get him to do his job for him. "There's a man at Deep Fork," the sergeant said casually. "You know where that is?"

"No."

"It's over in the Creek Nation, on the Deep Fork of the Canadian. Easy day's travel by horseback. The man's name is Otto Myer, he's a wildcatter. Ab Miller did a shootin' job for Myer in the Cherokee country about two months ago."

Concannon did some thinking. Six weeks ago, about

54

the time of the robbery, Miller was seen by Sam Speer and turned down a job. It might be interesting to talk to Otto Myer, who was probably Miller's last employer before the robbery. "How did you hear about this Myer?"

Bone shrugged. "Oklahoma City's got to be a congregatin' place for oil men. A policeman hears all kinds of things."

"Why don't *you* take this easy ride up to Deep Fork and talk to Myer?"

It was a foolish question. Bone smiled. "You know how it is on a city police force. Deep Fork's out of my territory—but there's nothin' keepin' a railroad agent from makin' the trip, if he felt like it."

It wasn't the innocent suggestion that it seemed, it was an order. Bone might be only a city police sergeant but he was in a position to make Concannon's life miserable, if he set his mind on it. "Would tomorrow be too late," Concannon asked dryly, "for me to start this little trip?"

"Tomorrow," the sergeant beamed, "would be fine."

CHAPTER 4

It was seven o'clock that night when Concannon appeared at the Fine and Dandy Cafe. Two cowhands were eating at one of the window tables; otherwise the place was empty of customers. Pat Duncan, the owner, met Concannon at the door with an unfriendly scowl. "Athena's in the kitchen gettin' her coat."

Concannon sat down at the counter. When Athena

Allard entered the dining room he got immediately to his feet and removed his hat—just as if he were accustomed to spending his time in genteel company instead of with madams and whores and police sergeants.

"I'm a little early," he said. "But I don't mind waitin'."

"No." She shook her head. "Pat's lettin' me go early tonight."

She was paler than Concannon remembered. There was worry in her eyes, and maybe even fear. Concannon said uncertainly, "I gathered from your note that you had somethin' to talk about in private. I rented a light rig; maybe we could go somewhere for supper?"

At first she didn't seem to understand him. Then she said, "No, I've eaten."

"I haven't. Is the food any good here?"

"Not very," she said with no hint of a smile. For a moment she closed her eyes and visibly gathered her thoughts. "You're right, I did want to talk to you in private. Not here. It's Pat—he's a good man, but he doesn't approve of . . ."

"Railroad agents," Concannon grinned. "A lot of people don't." He held the door for her and they went out under the jealous eyes of the cook.

They stood for a moment on the plankwalk and breathed the chill, smoky air of autumn evening. She looked at him and made herself smile, very faintly. "I'm sorry, Mr. Concannon. So much has happened, and I don't know how to tell . . ." She made a helpless gesture with her hands. "Are you really hungry?"

"It's been a busy day; I guess I forgot to eat."

56

"There's an ice-cream parlor on Main Street," she said slowly. "The best people go there."

Ice-cream parlor. The best people. Yes sir, he thought, that's the place for Marcus Concannon. It was only a short distance from the Fine and Dandy Cafe to Main Street, but as Concannon had already paid the rent on the buggy he felt that he ought to get some use out of it.

They rode the few blocks in silence. On West Second Street the whores were feeding the drunks tincture of opium and robbing them. In some dark corner of Bunco Alley a man might be dying violently. But there was no hint of that on Main Street. Concannon pulled up at the hitch rack in front of the Royal Confectionery and handed Athena Allard down.

Apparently a lot of people in Oklahoma City enjoyed ice cream. The place was crowded and there was a great deal of animated talk and laughter. Concannon caught a fleeting impression of blue serge suits, high stiff collars, and cameo stickpins. And lace chokers among the ladies, and piled-up hair stylings, and an over-all scent of lilac. To Concannon it was like stepping into another world. Marble-top tables and wire-back chairs. The cloying sweetness of vanilla and citrus and root beer herbs. The Royal Confectionery was, in its own way, as exotic as an opium den on Hop Boulevard.

For a moment Concannon tried to picture Lily Olsen in this setting. Suddenly he laughed, and Athena Allard looked at him sternly. A large waitress in a white smock moved toward them like a white cloud. "You'd better order for us," Concannon told Athena. "I haven't quite got the hang of ice-cream parlors."

She looked at him vacantly. "I know. Ray was always uncomfortable in such places." She told the girl to bring Concannon a dish of vanilla ice cream and some coconut cake, and she asked for a cherry phosphate for herself.

Coconut cake and ice cream. Concannon wondered what Marvin Bone would say to that, if he could have seen it. He sat back, looking admiringly at Athena Allard, waiting for her to tell why she had sent the note to his hotel. Her cheeks colored slightly. "I'm afraid you'll think I'm very foolish, Mr. Concannon. Perhaps even worse . . ."

He waved the thought away. "You can talk here as well as anywhere. Nobody's payin' any attention to us."

She looked at him. "Two men . . . came to see me last night."

Concannon froze. He saw the dead eyes of the pimp. The sheet-covered body of the dead prostitute. Suddenly it was as if they were in the middle of a desert alone, deaf to the gaiety of the Royal Confectionery, blind to the swirl of activity. After a moment he asked, "Where was this?"

"At my rooming house on North Broadway. They were waiting for me, I think, after I finished at the cafe. It was dark, about eight o'clock. They were waiting there behind the honeysuckle bush by the front gate."

"Did anybody else see them?"

She shook her head.

"What did they want?"

She looked straight at him. "I don't know if I did the

58

right thing by asking you to see me. I'm afraid it could make trouble for you. But I didn't know where else to go. And you did say that you were a friend of Ray's . . ."

"You did right," Concannon told her. "What did they want?"

"They . . . they wanted me to stop talkin' to you. They told me not to see you any more. They said if I did, somethin' bad would happen. But I didn't know what else to do . . ."

Concannon said quickly, "You did exactly right. Did they do . . . anything to hurt you?"

"One of them held me and kept his hand over my mouth, but they didn't hurt me."

"Can you describe them?"

She thought for a moment. "It was dark and I couldn't see them very well. They said . . ." She closed her eyes. "They said they had been friends of Ray's. But I had never seen them before. They said that Ray had helped them rob that train. And they said it wouldn't do anybody any good if I talked to you and made trouble. It would only drag Ray's good name through the mud. They said to think of all the years he had been a good lawman, and to let it go at that. And they asked me if I wanted to go through life known as the widow of an outlaw. Then they gave me this."

She took a familiar-looking package from her purse and put it on the table in front of Concannon. Cautiously, he unwrapped enough of the brown paper covering to see inside. It was a packet of crisp new greenbacks, exactly like the one the police had found in Maggie

Slatter's crib. "Have you counted it?"

Athena Allard nodded. "It's exactly two thousand dollars."

"What did they say when they gave it to you?"

"They said to take it and go away somewhere. Because Ray had been their friend, they didn't want to cause me any trouble."

The waitress brought the cake and ice cream and cherry phosphate. Suddenly Concannon wasn't hungry. There was a hard knot where his stomach was supposed to be. "What did they say after they gave you this package?"

"They told me again to go away from Oklahoma, that I couldn't bring Ray back to life. If I talked to you I would only make matters worse. What should I do with the money?"

"You could give it to the police."

"I thought of that. But those two men would soon find out about it, wouldn't they? And they would know that I didn't intend to do what they told me." She hesitated. "I'm afraid I didn't tell you everything. Even while they were threatening me I was trying to think where I could go for help. The only name I could think of was yours . . ." Spots of color appeared in her cheeks. "I told them you were in love with me."

Concannon was startled. "Why did you do that?"

"They were desperate men. They are prepared to kill you if you persist in your investigation. I wanted to convince them that you would drop it if I asked you to."

For the moment Concannon didn't try to add all that

up. "Well," he said, "you may be right about the police. Your two pals would be sure to find out about it. I could put the money in the company safe at the depot, if you want me to. He took a bite of the cake but did not taste it. "There's nothin' official about it, but there's a chance the company would let you keep part of it, if it helps solve the robbery and get back the rest of the money."

Something cold and hard looked at him from behind her eyes. "Mr. Concannon, I don't want that money. It makes me sick to touch it or think about it. If you don't understand that, then there is no use of our talking."

Concannon pulled back as if he had been slapped. "There are several things I don't understand, Mrs. Allard. Maybe you better tell me. What is it you want?"

"I want my husband's name cleared. That's all. Because you were his friend, I thought I could trust you. But I can't. Not if you believe he had anything to do with that robbery."

Concannon smiled a bit grimly. "The best way to clear Ray's name is to find the men who did commit the robbery. Have you ever seen this man before? He took out the tintype picture of Ab Miller and showed it to her.

She looked at it blankly. "No, I've never seen him. Who is he?"

"His name is Ab Miller. Did Ray ever mention anyone by that name?"

"Not that I remember. Why do you ask about him?"

"He's a nitroglycerin expert. Some people think he might be the one that blew the safe when the train was robbed."

She turned frigid again. Her back stiffened. "I see. I suppose you think that Ray and this man were friends. I suppose you think they were partners in robbing the train."

"Ma'am," Concannon said with flagging patience, "I'm tryin' not to think anything at all right now. I'm just askin' questions. Later I'll try to put it together." He pushed away the remains of the ice cream and cake.

When they were back in the buggy, he asked, "Do you think that cook at the cafe would be any good in case of a fight?"

She stared at him from a cool distance. "Why do you ask a thing like that?"

"Tomorrow I'm leavin' for the Creek Nation for a day or so. It may fool your two pals into thinkin' I've knocked off the job, or it may not. If it doesn't, you may need protection, and the best man for the job is Pat Duncan."

"Why Pat Duncan?"

"Because he's in love with you."

They rode for several seconds in silence. Then, looking straight ahead, she said, "Mr. Duncan is not a coward, if that is what you mean."

"Well, anyway . . ." Concannon shrugged. "Get him to pick you up in the mornin' and take you home after the cafe closes."

"He does that already . . . as a rule."

"But not last night, when the two men were waiting for you." They reached the noisy corner of Main and Broadway and Concannon turned north. Athena

Allard said quietly, "No, not last night."

"Would you mind telling me why?"

They rode on for several seconds. In the shadow of the raised buggy top her face was as pale as marble. "Last night," she said, "I went to be with Ray."

A cold finger went up Concannon's back. He stared at her. "Ray's dead. I didn't think there was ever any doubt about that."

"I know." She was looking away from him, talking to the night. "But sometimes . . . sometimes there is such an emptiness."

Concannon's mouth was dry. He licked his lips with the tip of his tongue. "Are you sayin' you went out to the cemetery last night? By yourself?"

"I hired a carriage. The driver waited for me."

After a moment Concannon cleared his throat and said: "Promise me somethin'. Promise you won't do that again—not until I get some things cleared up, anyhow."

She sat staring out at the night, her thoughts light-years away, with a dead man. When they came to Mrs. Robertson's frame rooming house she turned to Concannon and said, "If I have placed you in a position of danger, I'm sorry."

"That's all right, a certain amount of danger goes with the job."

"I know." She was back with Ray again for a moment. Then: "Are you going to help me clear Ray's name, Mr. Concannon?"

"I'm goin' to try. But until it's cleared it would be better if you took the advice of your two visitors and left Oklahoma City for a while."

"No. This is where Ray is. This is where I'll stay."

John Evers was at his desk in the depot office when Concannon returned from seeing Athena Allard to her rooming house. The division inspector was sitting back comfortably, gazing at the ceiling, one of his fine Cuban cigars in the corner of his mouth. He studied Concannon for a moment and said, "You look like hell."

"I feel like hell. They didn't keep you long at Fort Sill, did they?"

"Just long enough to get me back here in time to catch the next northbound to Chicago. Take my advice, Concannon, and don't let them make a division inspector out of you. What have you got there?"

Concannon dropped the brown paper packet on the desk. Evers looked at it and whistled. "Part of the grass money?"

"That's my guess." Concannon sank into the straight chair and, in a voice that was dull and tired, brought the inspector up to date.

"Well," Evers smiled pleasantly, 'another ninety-seven thousand, five hundred dollars, and you'll have the case cleared up. The company will be glad to hear you're making progress." He studied the tip of his perfectly burning cigar. "By the way, I'll be reporting to a board meeting in Chicago. They'll want to know how you're coming along with your investigation and how soon they can expect to hear the end of it."

You didn't argue with men like Evers. You simply listened politely and made agreeable sounds, and then you went out and did whatever was expected of you.

"It's my opinion," the inspector said, "that the key to your puzzle lies with Allard's widow. Lucky thing for all of us that she didn't take your advice to leave town. Work on her, Concannon. You're good at that sort of thing."

That was the second time in two days that he had been told that he was good at that kind of thing; it was a phrase that he was beginning to get tired of. "She's still in love with Ray," he said coldly. "I think she always will be."

Evers smiled away the suggestion. "Women are the most changeable of God's creatures, and on the subject of love they're the most changeable of all. Just stay with her and keep her talking. Sooner or later she'll place the key right in your hand." He stood up and stretched with immense satisfaction.

"Maybe," Concannon said acidly, "while I'm keepin' company with Mrs. Allard and lookin' for the key, you can tell me how I keep those two hardcases from killin' both of us."

"You're an experienced lawman, Concannon. You know how to handle these things. In the meantime I suggest you try to locate that explosives expert, Miller. If Marvin Bone thinks you ought to make a trip to the Creek country, then you'd better do it. Bone usually knows what he's talking about."

"He's also pretty good at gettin' other folks to do his work for him."

Evers smiled absently. In the distance the Santa Fe northbound was approaching the south switches. "I've got to be going now, Concannon. I'll tell the board members that they can expect results within a matter of days."

Evers walked out of the office, leaving the fragrance of rich Cuban tobacco behind him. Concannon continued to sit on the visitors side of the desk. He was sore and bruised and tired to the bone. He thought about Athena Allard. "Sometimes there is such an emptiness," she had said. And there she stood, in his mind, beside the new grave of her husband. The thought of it made Concannon shiver.

With an effort he shook himself free of that melancholy thought. Best to stick to practical things—such as staying alive. And keeping Athena alive. He gave some thought to her two night visitors. They were probably sitting back now, waiting to see what would happen next. Tomorrow morning when they saw Concannon pulling out of Oklahoma City, maybe they would think Athena had succeeded in getting him to quit the case. Or, he thought darkly, maybe they would have second thoughts on the subject and decide to kill them both. A rifle from a second story window. A knife in some dark alleyway. Another reception at Mrs. Robertson's honeysuckle bush.

There was not much way to stop a killing once a murderer had made his mind up on the matter. Ask the pimp. Or Maggie Slatter.

The Day and Night was going full blast. Smoke and

noise and barely controlled hysteria hit Concannon in the face as he stepped inside. All the tables were busy, the bar was crowded, Lily's three girls were going up and down the stairs with their customers. Everything was just as it ought to be, except that Marvin Bone wasn't in his usual chair, back to the wall, watching the door. He was standing at the bar.

Concannon went straight to the bar and took a place beside the policeman. "What's your name?" he asked the new bartender.

"Bob Polk, Mr. Concannon."

And a smart young man you are, too, Concannon thought. Knows how to show proper respect to the owner's special friends. Nice appearance, ready smile, and he was probably stealing Lily blind. A man like that had a bright future on Bunco Alley. "Bob, Miss Olsen keeps a special bottle down there on the bottom shelf. Would you move it up here, please?"

"Yes sir, Mr. Concannon." He put the bottle on the bar and industriously polished a glass to go beside it. Concannon filled the glass to the brim and drained it. Only then did he look at Sergeant Bone.

"It's not my habit to offer good Tennessee whiskey to policemen, but . . ."

Bone grimaced as if he had tasted a green persimmon. "You know better'n that, Concannon."

Concannon shrugged and refilled his own glass. He drank to the policeman's iron-rigid honesty and the slickness of Lily's bartenders. It was comforting to know that some things never changed. He set down the empty glass.

"You're goin' at that pretty hard," the sergeant said sourly.

"I've got the taste of coconut cake to get out of my mouth."

"You talked to Allard's widow tonight. What about?"

The fine old whiskey sent comforting waves of warmth to distant parts of Concannon's body. Cramped muscles began to relax. Gradually, the world was becoming a sunnier place to live in. He was sorely tempted to tell Bone to go to hell and mind his own business, but because of the whiskey he said, "Later, Bone, later. I'm sick of business tonight."

"Are you goin' to talk to that wildcatter I told you about?"

"Otto Myer. I remember the name well." He was becoming lightheaded, which was not surprising considering that he had eaten nothing but a few bites of coconut cake in the past twenty-four hours. "Yes, I aim to talk to Mr. Myer tomorrow, if I can find him."

"I told you where to find him."

"I remember." He refilled his glass.

"When will you be goin'?"

"First thing in the mornin'. You can do me a favor, Bone, while I'm away. Keep an eye on Mrs. Allard."

The policeman looked at him sharply. "Why?"

"There are folks that think Ray had somethin' to do with the robbery. Maybe they think the same about her. Anyway, I'd rest easier if I knew you were keepin' an eye on her."

The lawman shrugged. "All right."

Concannon debated briefly on whether to tell him about Athena Allard's two visitors. But if he did that he would have to tell him about the money, and within a matter of hours everybody would know that Ray Allard's widow had rejected the bribe and that would be dangerous. Sooner or later, of course, the police would have to know. But not now. With a little luck he would locate Ab Miller and get to the bottom of the mess, and Athena would no longer be in any danger.

Concannon downed another glass of Lily's Tennessee whiskey. Something rubbed against his leg. It was Satan. He picked the cat up and sat it on the bar and said to the bartender, "Bob, set up a saucer of milk for my pal here." He was definitely drunk. Not falling-down, brawling drunk, but warmly and pleasantly drunk. It was a strange sensation because whiskey did not usually affect him that way.

Bob Polk, the perfect bartender, got a saucer of milk and set it in front of Satan, as though serving cats at the bar was the commonest thing in the world. Bone watched the little demonstration with undisguised disgust, then turned and left the saloon.

"Drink 'er up," Concannon told the cat, "there's plenty more where that came from."

Satan licked the saucer clean then sat looking at Concannon and washing his face. There was something in the back of Concannon's mind wanting out. But he locked the door on it. He poured himself some more whiskey. He was about to down it when Lily Olsen appeared beside him and said, "I never realized before that you were such a serious drinker."

"You're the second one tonight," Concannon told her pleasantly, "to comment on that subject. How about gettin' another glass and let's take the bottle upstairs."

"I can't now, I've got to talk business to one of the town councilmen." She looked at him with concern. "Are you sure you're all right?"

"I'm fine, Lily. Don't mother me."

She shrugged. "Why don't you take the bottle upstairs and wait for me. I won't be long."

He saluted her soberly. "A good idea. A fine idea." He tucked Satan under one arm, picked up the bottle, and walked cautiously to the stairway.

For some time Concannon wandered about Lily's sitting room, touching familiar items on the tables, staring blindly at the colored lithographs on the wall. Satan curled up on a French settee and went to sleep. Concannon poured himself a drink. Then it came over him suddenly, like a flood from a breaking dam. He was seized by a longing that he didn't immediately understand. It was stronger than an alcoholic's craving for whiskey, stronger than a starving man's hunger for food.

He stared at the cat and said aloud, "Lord help me, I think I'm in love."

For a moment he saw Athena Allard as if she were with him there in the room, and he wanted her more than he had ever wanted a woman before, but in a different way. She was looking at him but not seeing him. That is the way it would always be. Athena Allard would never be able to see any man but her husband. And Ray was dead.

When Lily entered the room Concannon was sitting on one of the needlepoint chairs gazing idly at the empty bottle. She looked at him with affection and sighed: "Concannon, do you want to tell me about it?"

"There's nothin' much to tell. I'm drunk. I better go to the hotel tonight."

"You're not the first man I've seen that's had too much to drink. I'll turn down the bed."

Slowly, he shook his head. "No, I better not."

She didn't understand at first; she thought he was afraid of making a fool of himself in bed, because of too much whiskey. "Nonsense," she told him briskly, "you'll stay here, like you always do when you're in town. It doesn't matter about the liquor."

She frowned. Slowly she understood that their relationship had changed. She didn't know just how, but her woman's instincts told her that Concannon was somehow a different man. She sat on the settee next to Satan and the big cat purred contentedly as she stroked it. "I'll be damned," she said after a moment. "It's a woman, isn't it?"

Concannon made a weak attempt to smile. "Crazy, ain't it?"

"It's one thing I hadn't figured on. I always knew the time would come when the trail would fork and you'd go your own way, but I always figured it would be the railroad and your job that would separate us. Somehow I hadn't counted on a woman." After a

71

moment she asked, "Do I know her?"

"I don't know. I don't think so."

But she knew. There was very little that happened in Oklahoma City that Lily Olsen didn't know about. She took a few rumors that she had heard, added them to a fact or two that she was sure about, and counted it up, like a poker hand. The answer was Athena Allard.

She shook her head slowly. Being a gambler herself she could sense the beginning of a losing streak. "It won't work, Concannon."

"I guess not," he admitted.

"Ray was your friend. You've told me a dozen times how he saved your life. He'll always be standin' there between you."

"I know. But it doesn't make any difference."

"Well," she said, smiling bleakly, "I'm too old a hand to start makin' a racket or anything like that." She got his hat from a nearby table and handed it to him. "Goodbye, Concannon."

There didn't seem to be anything else to say. Concannon took his hat and left.

CHAPTER 5

The next morning Concannon went to the livery stables on South Broadway to select a saddle animal. "Take the gray gelding," said Detective Sergeant Marvin Bone as he crossed from the barn to the rent corral. "I know the man that owned him before the livery stable got him."

"Bone," Concannon said wearily, "don't you have

anything to do except watch over me all the time?"

The policeman showed his teeth in what he supposed to be a smile. "Just seein' you don't get the worst of it in rent animals. You headed for Creek country?"

"At the urging of the Oklahoma City Police Department and John Evers."

"The trip'll be worth the trouble if you learn anything about that well shooter."

"And if I don't?"

"Nothin' ventured, nothin' gained, like they say."

Concannon selected the gray gelding and helped the stablehand get it saddled. "Bone, you won't forget to keep an eye on Mrs. Allard, will you?"

"I won't forget. Anything special I ought to look out for?"

Yes, two of the men who probably robbed the Santa Fe express car. But he didn't say it.

"You holdin' somethin' back from me, Concannon?" Bone said casually.

". . . No"

Uncharacteristically, the policeman shrugged away his natural curiosity. "Talk to that wildcatter, Myer. If anybody can tell you about Ab Miller, he's the one."

Concannon rode north on Broadway, past the landscaped lawns and big houses of Oklahoma City's new society. Within a short time he was in open country, slanting up the long northern slope of the Canadian River Valley. By midafternoon he had crossed the North Fork of the Canadian and was well into Creek country.

Here the land was gently rolling hills, tawny in

autumn. The yellow leaves of cottonwoods sparkled in the sun, the blood red of sweet gum leaves began to appear in the bottoms. Concannon tasted the cleanness of the air and noted the unscarred earth and glittering streams . . . but vaguely. His mind was somewhere else.

He kept seeing the dirty dead face of the pimp. And the carelessly wrapped bundle that had been Maggie Slatter. It could as easily have been Athena. He began to sweat; his clothing became clammy against his skin. Common sense told him that he was doing the right thing in trying to locate Miller. That was one thing that everybody seemed to agree on—the explosives expert was the key to the robbery. But that didn't make it any easier to ride off and leave Athena in a city with two men who had already killed twice.

The sun was about two hours high and Concannon judged that he was still half a day from Deep Fork. Bone had been too optimistic in his estimation of the distance. And the gray gelding was a rangy, hard-gaited animal that soon had Concannon's spine numb from the constant jarring—Bone had been too optimistic on that score too.

In the distance he raised a thin line of timber marking a stream. Concannon put the gelding into a brown valley between two shaggy knolls, making for the water, when the animal suddenly took a curious, single-footed little hop and fell. Only after the animal started to fall did Concannon hear the rifle.

The horse dropped like a rock, and Concannon kicked savagely to free his feet of the stirrups before crashing to the ground. His mind for the moment was eerily blank. As the animal was falling his only thought was the useless regret that he had not thought to bring a rifle with him.

The gelding fell with a grunt and lay kicking, snorting bright, frothy blood into the brown grass. Concannon landed several feet away, rolling, bumping over the rough sod, but he was hardly aware of that. His hat fell off and instinctively he grabbed for it. A bullet snatched the hat out of his hands, like a hawk snapping up a fieldmouse. He let the hat go and continued to roll freely away from the gelding. His snub-barreled .38 was still in its shoulder holster, and he let it stay there. With the riflemen almost two hundred yards away, a pistol was not going to help him.

At some point, between the time he left the saddle and hit the ground, he realized there were two riflemen instead of one. One on each of the two knolls that guarded the small valley. Comin' back to finish the job you started in the alley, are you? he thought coldly.

These were idle, passing thoughts, flashing like summer lightning in his mind, entirely removed from the eruption of violence, the distant crack of rifles, the blood-chilling hissing of bullets. In the meantime the gelding had kicked a few times, weakly, and then lay still. Concannon was racing zigzag away from that flat, bald area where the gelding had fallen, away from that bullet-swept area of most immediate danger.

From the time he hit the ground to the time he dived into the rattling, prickly thicket of wild plum bushes, no more than ten seconds could have passed. It might have been ten lifetimes. Or, he thought grimly, ten deathtimes. The riflemen were firing furiously, frustrated and angered at having missed their target at the beginning. A cooler head would have paused a second, taken a deep breath, aimed carefully, and that would have been the end of it.

Concannon scrambled out of the thicket into a stand of dead mullein. Bullets ripped through the plum bushes seconds after he had vacated the spot. He crawled behind an outcrop and lay there panting, listening, watching, sniffing.

The firing stopped. A thoughtful silence settled over the twin knolls. The hunters and the hunted all paused to take stock.

Concannon's only consolation was that he was still alive. The riflemen still had their weapons, and they were wiser and less excited. Killing a trained lawman was not quite the same as murdering a pimp or a Second Street whore, but it was still a simple matter. All they had to do was wait for Concannon to reveal himself.

It was a good plan, except that the sun lay close to the western horizon and the time they could spend on waiting was limited.

Concannon lay like a lizard behind the outcrop, his eyes moved watchfully from side to side, his breathing shallow. He lay near the base of the western knoll, which was already in shadow. The rifleman was up above somewhere, but Concannon could not see him. Across the bare defile the second knoll was a jumble of grass and brush and rocks and outcrops—no rifleman that Concannon could see. But he was there. Concannon had two neat, black, .30-caliber holes in the sleeve of his canvas windbreaker to prove it.

He regarded those holes for a moment. The bullet had entered the windbreaker just below the elbow and exited two inches above, without touching his arm. It was pleasant to think that he was not now gritting his teeth in pain, his life pouring out of a mangled arm. But, as a sometime gambler, it was disturbing to think of so much luck used up so quickly.

The rifleman on the slope above Concannon began to move cautiously in Concannon's direction. There was no sign of life on the opposite knoll—not that it mattered. The rifleman could have stood up in the hard, direct sunlight and waved his arms; there was nothing Concannon could have done about it with a pistol.

A voice from above said, "Concannon, you just won't listen to reason, will you?" It was a voice that wheezed slightly and sounded as if it came from the depths of a big chest. The last time Concannon had heard it was in the alleyway alongside the Day and Night.

"We tried to convince you the nicest way we could," the voice went on disappointedly, "that you wouldn't be smart to think too much about that oil well shooter. But you wouldn't listen. You're just naturally bullheaded, I'm beginnin' to think. One of these days it's goin' to get you killed." He chuckled. "And today's the day, Concannon."

He was moving slowly, almost silently, down the face

of the slope. Then he stopped for a minute, listening. "Concannon, you hear me?"

Concannon made no sound. He lay hard against the rock. His double-action .38 was in his hand, which surprised him slightly. He didn't remember taking it out of its holster.

"Concannon?"

Mister, Concannon thought, I've got some questions I sure enough would like to put to you—they're inside me throbbin' like a rotten tooth. But I don't think I'll ask them now, if it's all the same to you.

"That was a right fancy little jig you done runnin' across the flat," the rifleman said with amusement. "Not much wonder that me and Croy missed you." There was a moment of silence. "Or *did* we miss you? Is that your trouble, Concannon? Are you laid up with a bullet in your gut, like an old coyote in his den, waitin' to die?"

Why don't you come down and see for yourself? Concannon thought. For a long while neither of them made a sound. The shadow of the knoll stretched darkly out and touched the dead gelding. Within a few minutes it had reached the base of the knoll where Croy waited. Concannon tried to remember if he knew anybody by the name of Croy. He didn't.

Suddenly a rifle roared from almost directly above. The loudness and nearness of it caused Concannon to jump. The bullet struck a rock and went screaming up toward the blue sky. Instinctively, Concannon almost leaped to his feet and started running.

That was what the rifleman had been hoping for. A full

minute passed and there wasn't a sound as the rifleman waited for Concannon to reveal himself. There was a tense, electric anticipation in the air. Concannon could almost hear it crackle. He pressed against the outcrop and sweated and did not move.

At last the rifleman chuckled resignedly. "You're a cool one, Concannon. I got to give you that much. Either that or you're too hurt to move, or you're dead." He sighed. Concannon could hear him snapping cartridges in the magazine of his rifle. The shadow was almost halfway up the opposite knoll. Within another hour it would be dark. They would still be two against one, and they would still have rifles. But hitting a moving target at nighttime was going to make it more difficult for them.

There was movement on the opposite knoll. Croy was tired of waiting. He had decided to get his horse and come over and see what was going on.

"Well," the familiar voice said, still unruffled, "I can't say that I blame you for wantin' to play possum with us, Concannon, but in the end we'll dig you out. Don't fret about that."

Concannon heard the sound of hoofs. Croy was circling around to the north, getting ready to join his pal. Then they would set up a crossfire pattern and shoot him out. If they worked fast they had plenty of time to do it before sundown.

Comfortable as it is behind this outcrop, Concannon told himself grimly, you've got to find yourself a better place to hide. But he didn't move. He could no longer hear Croy's horse, so he could only guess that the second rifleman had staked his animal at a safe distance and was coming the rest of the way on foot.

Concannon moved his hand along the ground, found a small pebble and flipped it straight ahead. The rifleman on the upper slope chuckled at this feeble attempt to trick him. "You'll have to think of somethin' better'n that, Concannon. And you haven't got much time to do it in."

Concannon studied the lengthening shadows but was not comforted. The riflemen still have plenty of time. He took a deep breath and sighed a little in resignation. The time for lying shivering behind rocks and waiting for the inevitable had passed; this was the time to do something. In the pit of his stomach there was an aching void, but at least he had stopped sweating. His mind was calm.

He flipped another pebble. Then, as the rifleman was beginning to chuckle superiorly, Concannon lunged up from the outcrop firing the .38 as fast as he could pull the trigger.

The rifleman was startled by the suddenness of Concannon's suicidal rush. After a brief hesitation, he wheeled and fired. The rifle bellowed, almost in Concannon's face, but the bullet ripped through a patch of weeds and went screaming off across the prairie. Concannon continued to claw his way up the slope, firing until the revolver was empty. He threw himself at a pair of brown boots.

For a moment a wildness seized him. He imagined that he remembered those boots—those hard, sharp-toed boots that had slammed repeatedly into his ribs that night alongside Lily's saloon. He imagined that he could even remember the detail of fancy stitching above the vamps, and the worn places on the inside where they have rubbed stirrup leather. In a cooler part of his mind he realized that such well-remembered detail was highly unlikely, but that did not lessen the savagery of his attack.

The man grunted, first in surprise, then in fear, as Concannon knocked his feet from under him and both went crashing down the face of the knoll.

In the distance Concannon heard the second rifleman's alarmed shouting. At the moment he had a more immediate interest. The two men, locked together, slammed into a stump of scrub spruce, and Concannon's breath went out of him. With the outlaw's hands about Concannon's throat, both men went off a shelf and crashed to the ground below. Concannon glimpsed the rifle flying slowly, gracefully through the air. The hands on his throat tightened. Blindly, Concannon struck with the short barrel of his pistol.

The man went limp. The choking fingers fell away. For what must have been several seconds Concannon lay with murder in his eyes and started to get to his knees. Concannon raised himself to his elbow and hit him again with the pistol barrel.

The second rifleman—Croy—was hollering excitedly from someplace near the top of the knoll. "What the hell's goin' on here! Turk, you all right?"

Turk was not all right; there was a gash alongside his head, above his left ear, and a considerable amount of blood was smeared on that side of his face. He lay with his face in gravel and was probably experiencing a great deal of pain. But he was alive.

Concannon was bruised and shaken, and his windbreaker had been torn in the scramble, but he was in better shape than Turk. He crawled toward his attacker, quickly slipped the single-action .45 out of his holster and prodded him with the barrel. "Come alive, mister. You got some talkin' to do."

From up above Croy was still hollering. Concannon ignored him, grabbed Turk by his collar and pulled him beneath the shelf where they wouldn't be so exposed.

All that took considerable effort, and when it was over Concannon fell back against the clay wall gasping for breath. He looked around for Turk's lost rifle, but it was nowhere in sight. He prodded the gunman with the .45.

"Your pal's callin' you, Turk. It's time you let him know how you are."

Turk opened one eye, turned over on his back and looked at Concannon with blazing hatred. His hand jumped immediately to his empty holster. Concannon grinned and showed him the .45.

The man called Turk was red-haired, blue-eyed, and had a skin so fair that his face was always sunburned, even in October. Concannon could almost have guessed his name from looking at him; half of the red-haired men west of Chicago were known as Turk or Turkey Red. "Turk," Concannon said meaningfully, cocking the heavy revolver, "holler up to your pal and tell him to stay where he is."

Turk spat an obscenity. But when Concannon began to swing with the .45 he quickly decided to cooperate. The left side of Turk's face was becoming extraordinarily sensitive to pistol barrels.

"Stay where you are, Croy, he's got the drop on me!"

Concannon smiled. "That's better. Now there are a few questions I want answered. Who are you and why did you go to so much trouble to kill me? You could have done it a lot easier the other night in Oklahoma City."

Turk looked at him with bitterness that was cold and deadly. "If I'd had my way about it, I *would* of killed you then." Immediately he realized that he had already said too much. He locked his heavy jaws and glared.

Concannon shrugged. "As you can see, you'd have been right. Who was it that stopped you? Croy?"

Turk spat at the ground to show what he thought of that suggestion. "Somebody else, then," Concannon went on. "The boss of the bunch that took the grass money?"

"You're wastin' your breath, Concannon."

"Was it Ab Miller, the nitroglycerin expert?"

Turk sneered. High on the knoll Croy was hollering again but Concannon ignored him. "This is your chance to be smart, Turk. The railroad knows that Ab Miller was in the bunch. Now we know about you and Croy. The whole scheme is fallin' apart. Get out of it while you can."

Turk was beginning to look bored. He merely yawned when Concannon said, "The railroad wants that money bad. There might be a reward if you cooperated in gettin' it back."

Turk wiped his bloody face on his sleeve and said nothing. "How did you know where to lay the ambush today?" Concannon asked. "Somebody must have told you I was investigatin' Miller."

The big outlaw gazed angrily into space. He might have been stone-deaf for all the attention he was giving Concannon's questions. For a moment Concannon tried to remember how many people had known about his trip to the Creek Nation. Lily? He couldn't remember whether he had mentioned it to her. Bone? Athena Allard? They were the only ones he could think of.

Concannon became aware of the silence that had settled on the knoll. Croy had stopped his hollering and was instead slowly making his way down the slope. With a quick look at Turk, Concannon said, "Tell your pal to stay where he is or I'll kill you."

Something in the grimness of the situation caused Turk to laugh unpleasantly. "You don't reckon Croy'd do much cryin' if I got myself killed, do you? It'd just mean there'd be more of the grass money for him and . . ."

"Him and who?" Concannon asked quickly.

But Turk only grinned.

"All right . . ." Concannon looked at the outlaw along the barrel of the revolver and quietly began adding pressure to the trigger. Turk maintained his indifference for perhaps a second, then he began to sweat. "Croy!" he hollered hoarsely. "He's goin' to kill me if you come any closer!"

There was a moment when both men held their breaths. There was no sound from the top of the knoll. If

Croy was moving at all he was doing it very quietly and slowly. "See there," Concannon said dryly. "There's friendship in the world, after all."

"Friendship!" Turk spat viciously into the dry mullein. "He knows our chances of killin' you are twice as good as long as we're both alive."

Concannon eased the pressure on the trigger. "That bein' the case, have you figured your chances when all this is over? Are you sure you'll ever get your part of that grass money?"

Turk looked at him poisonously, and Concannon took note of the small fact that he had learned. For some reason, the loot from the robbery had not yet been divided—which was probably the reason for the gang's remaining in the Oklahoma Territory.

The sun settled slowly behind the wooded hills of the Creek Nation. A time of half daylight settled on the land, a gray dusk that absorbed all color and warmth and life. A flight of bullbats swooped over the knoll, their white-striped wings cutting gracefully through the heavy air. A smoky, silent end to a violent day. But the violence wasn't over yet. That was too much to hope for, with Croy still alive and active on top of the knoll.

Concannon looked down at the dead gelding. Somebody would have to account to the livery stable for the loss of the animal and rig, and Concannon had no doubts about who that somebody would be. A month's pay, and nothing to show for it except a dead horse, a number of cuts and bruises, and some damaged clothing.

He found himself thinking about Ray Allard. Ray of

the handsome face and ready laugh. Ray, the bosom friend of dance-hall girls from the Platte to the Bravo. A first-class lawman, brave almost to the point of being suicidal. A good man to ride with. Concannon was living proof of that.

Concannon had laughed when he first heard of Ray's marriage. One of those dance-hall girls had finally trapped him, he thought. He had not been prepared for anyone like Athena. What had a woman like her seen in Ray? The same things the dance-hall girls had seen in him, most likely, although Concannon found that thought unusually disagreeable.

Turk was watching him closely, waiting for a moment of carelessness, a moment when Concannon's mind would be occupied with other things, and then . . . Concannon looked at him coldly. "Don't try it, mister. Sit easy and count your blessings, that's the best thing for you right now."

The dead gray light was slowly bleeding out of the sky. It had been some time since they had heard from Croy.

Concannon thought about Athena Allard. Her face haunted him. The childlike directness of her eyes. Her bitterness and fear and sense of emptiness—all of it was in her eyes. She had never learned to keep her feelings hidden, never learned the art of deception. Which was why Concannon knew that it was hopeless. When she looked at him he could see exactly what she thought of him—nothing. He was merely a tool with which she hoped to clear the name of her husband. A tool to be used once and then discarded.

Concannon was aware of all these things, and still it made no difference. When he thought of her he got as moon-eyed as the greenest greenhorn staring at a theater poster of Lily Langtry. He was disgusted with himself.

But he didn't know what to do about it.

Turk was now watching him closer than ever. For a minute it was almost as if shades had been drawn behind Concannon's eyes. They were curiously vacant and staring. What he was thinking about Turk didn't know, and he didn't care. All he needed was a second, a small part of a second, to jump, to knock the .45 out of Concannon's hands, to grab it away from him. With luck, it would be all over in a matter of three or four seconds.

But it was not Turk's lucky day. He lunged and Concannon drew back for an instant in mild surprise. Then, coldly and calmly, he swung the heavy .45.

The outlaw fell as if he had been poleaxed. He lay with his face in the gravel, not even twitching. Concannon quickly went down on one knee and felt the large artery beneath Turk's jaw. The beat of life was still there. The outlaw's head may never be quite the same again, but he was still alive.

Concannon shoved Turk's .45 into his waistband and stood very still, listening to the night. Where are you, Croy? Are you still here on the knoll? Have you moved off someplace to lay another trap for me? Do you care what has happened to your partner?

Croy didn't say. The night, except for the whispering sounds of small scurrying things, was silent.

Concannon looked at the still figure of the outlaw. He

didn't feel sorry for him, but he felt almost even with him for the beating he had taken in Bunco Alley. "Probably," he said to himself, "I'll regret it later that I didn't kill you when I had the chance." Then he began easing his way down to the base of the knoll.

Where the night had gone to, Concannon could not remember. He dimly recalled crawling for what seemed like miles, over gravel and through briars and stands of dry weeds. Once he thought he heard the sound of horses. Croy had apparently brought his pal to life again and they were back on the job. A little late and a little the worse for wear, but on the job.

It occurred to Concannon that he was not doing so well himself. Set afoot in the middle of Creek country. Two mounted assassins—with rage in their hearts, no doubt—looking for him.

He came to the stream that he had glimpsed in the distance before Croy and Turk had tried to kill him. Too exhausted to care about how much noise he made, he blundered through brush and fell gasping beside the water. He drank his fill and then lay there at the edge of the stream waiting for the hammering in his chest to subside. He cursed himself for ever complaining about that hard-gaited gelding. He thought now of the animal as a dear and old friend—but a friend now dead and of no use to him at all.

After a while he began to think more clearly. What he needed was a horse. When daylight came he couldn't hope to outrun or outdodge two mounted riflemen. But where could a man with little money and no friends get a horse?

The answer to that was relatively simple. He would steal one.

As a lawman, the prospect of going into the horse-stealing business was not a pleasant one. For one thing, horse thieves often came to unpleasant ends. On the other hand, his future as a hunted man on foot was even more unpleasant. That settled, the thing now was to find a horse.

Not a simple matter; not at night, and with only a vague idea as to where he was. There were Creek settlements throughout the Nation, but to start his horse-stealing career in a settlement of Indians didn't seem a very promising beginning. An Indian farm was the logical place to look. If he knew where to find a farm.

He lay for some time, his mind blank. Then, as his exhaustion receded, his thoughts became clearer. Farms needed water. And the best farmland was bottomland near a stream. All he had to do was start walking along this stream and sooner or later he would find a Creek farm and, hopefully, a horse.

Sooner or later.

The longer he thought about it the more transparent the scheme seemed to him. Turk and Croy were sure to think of the same thing. By daylight they would pick up his trail and . . .

Concannon didn't want to think about that. From his vest pocket he took a box of .38 caliber cartridges and reloaded his double-action revolver. He had no ammunition for Turk's .45, but there were five rounds in the cylinder. He shoved the heavy weapon back into his waistband, pulled himself to his feet and started walking.

Once he glimpsed two horsemen riding northwest along the timbered stream. Whether they were Turk and Croy, he couldn't tell, but an ache in his gut said they were. He wondered if Turk had found his rifle.

He walked for what seemed a long time, fighting his way through dense undergrowth. Once he tripped over a tangle of possum grapevines and fell sprawling. He lay there panting and sweating and cursing the day he had allowed himself to take a job as a railroad detective. He had forgotten what the life of a deputy United States marshal could be like. Twice the danger at half the pay. He shoved himself to his feet and continued on to the north, upstream, deeper into the heart of Creek country.

The two horsebackers did not show themselves again, and he began to breathe a little easier. Maybe they hadn't been Turk and Croy after all. Maybe the two would-be assassins had decided to quit and go home, wherever that was. Maybe the sun would rise in the west.

About two hours before first light he came to a small Indian settlement there on the bank of the stream. A cluster of small stockade houses stood silent and forlorn in the clearing. Nothing moved. If there were any horses they were in the lean-to sheds that stood alongside the houses. Concannon decided that he did not want a horse bad enough to go up to an Indian's house and try to steal one. Besides, there was sure to be one or two Indian Light Horse policemen in a settlement of this size. If the horse owner didn't catch him, the Creek policemen would.

Wearily, he backtrailed downstream, waded to the other side and circled the settlement. By the time he had the place behind him the first frosty light of dawn was beginning to show in the east.

He sat on a fallen cottonwood to get his breath. He wished for hot coffee and flapjacks and eggs and maybe a piece of fried steak on the side. What he had was nothing. Not even a piece of jerky to still his growling stomach.

He walked. As the eastern light began to spread he became alarmed. Horse-stealing at any time was a touchy business; horse-stealing from an Indian in broad daylight was suicidal. Maybe he had made a mistake in bypassing the settlement. Not that it made any difference now. It was too late to go back.

By the time he finally raised a farm the hazy, iron-hard light of early morning lay on the creek bottom. Concannon lay on his stomach on a bed of dry leaves and studied the situation in dismay. There was the familiar stockade house, a good-sized barn, and several smaller sheds of the brush arbor variety. An impressive layout by Creek standards. Beyond the house there was a fairly large field of corn stubble—the grain had already been harvested. A flock of guineas roved nervously in the yard in front of the house. A dog barked irritably.

Concannon groaned to himself. A flock of noisy guineas and an ill-tempered dog. For a beginning horse thief the signs couldn't be worse.

Still he lay there beneath the bony arms of a giant cottonwood. The Indian farmer came out of the house, stretched, yawned, scratched himself and gazed up at the sky. A woman called to him and he went back into the house.

Concannon's heart sank. On a farm of this size he knew there would be at least two work animals in the barn—or possibly in a horse lot on the other side of the barn. But they could not help him now.

He was about to backtrack again, circle the farm and continue on upstream, when the nervous guineas suddenly began to scatter in a raucous storm of sound. Two horse-backers rode out of a stand of timber to the west of the house and reined toward the dooryard. They were Turk and Croy.

The Indian came out of the house. A woman and three small children followed; the children clung to the man's legs.

Concannon was not comforted to see that Turk wore his hat cautiously on one side of his head and that the left side of his face was swollen and discolored. The outlaw's pale eyes glinted like hard-edged stones in the early light. Also, a walnut stock showed clearly in Turk's cutaway saddle scabbard—he had found his rifle.

There was nothing at all about the red-haired outlaw to ease Concannon's anxiety. He turned his attention to the second rifleman, the one called Croy.

Croy was a lanky, awkward, rawboned man. He sat his saddle slouched and heavy, in a way that would soon gall the back of any horse he rode. There was little expression in his slablike face, yet he gave Concannon the impression of being quietly desperate.

The two outlaws began shooting questions at the Indian. The Creek shrugged and answered them in careful, missionary school English. Concannon, from his position on the creek bank, could not hear what was being said, but he could guess.

In a sudden flare of anger, Turk leaned far out of the saddle and snarled something in the Indian's face. The Creek farmer merely shrugged and shook his head. Both outlaws shot questions at him, but the farmer, who had been friendly enough at first, began to freeze. Suddenly Turk, the hotheaded one of the pair, grabbed his rifle out of the saddle boot and aimed it at the Indian's chest.

The man looked at Turk and didn't even blink. He grunted something to the woman and she quietly disappeared into the house, taking the children with her.

Turk began cursing the Indian savagely, the muzzle of his rifle pressed against his chest. The farmer seemed steadily to grow taller and colder and more silent. At last Croy took Turk's arm and said something to him. Grudgingly, Turk pulled away with the rifle and shoved it back into the boot. Showing an unexpected sense of diplomacy, Croy seemed to be trying to soothe the Indian's ruffled dignity.

The Creek farmer merely looked at them. He was clearly in no mood to be soothed.

Finally the two riflemen pulled back a few paces and held a brief conference. Then they made a quick scout of the house and the barn and the sheds. In a rage, Turk made one more snarling remark to the Indian before Croy finally hazed him out of the farmyard. They disappeared into the timber.

The Indian stood for some time in front of his house; beneath his brown skin there was a pallor of gray. The frightened woman called to him, but he stood there for another five minutes, staring at the place where the outlaws had entered the timber. At last he turned and went into the house.

Concannon breathed a deep sigh of relief. He was safe—for a little while. His situation hadn't improved, but at least he was alive—and that was getting to be more important all the time. He sat for a moment, making himself think quietly and calmly, trying to decide what to do next. One thing he wasn't going to do, and that was try to steal a horse from the angry farmer.

After a few minutes the Indian came out of the house again, this time with a shotgun in his hands. Concannon's anxiety returned. The farmer came straight toward him. He could see the shotgun's cocked hammer and the brown finger on the trigger. The muzzle of the weapon seemed to grow steadily as it came closer. When it was as big as the mouth of a tunnel, the Indian stopped.

"Come out. I know you are there."

The Creek spoke slowly and carefully—his anger was not in his voice but in the smoldering fire behind his eyes. There was one rule of survival that Concannon was always careful to observe; never argue with a shotgun. He stood up and came toward the Indian.

"How did you know I was here?"

"I saw the crows flying away when you came upstream."

Concannon smiled ruefully. That's what came of riding in trains and living in hotels for five years—a man forgot. "Then you knew I was here all the time, even while the two horsebackers were questionin' you."

It was the Indian's turn to shrug. He moved his shotgun slightly so that it wasn't aimed quite at the center of Concannon's chest. "You know the two horsemen?"

"Well enough." Concannon had already made up his mind to tell the Creek anything he wanted to know and hope for the best. "They robbed a train down in the Chickasaw Nation—at least, I think they did. They've decided that I know more about them than's good for them, so they've got their minds made up to kill me."

The Indian accepted this with another shrug. "Who are you?"

"Marcus Concannon, I'm a railroad detective."

The Indian scowled. "Government law?"

The deputy U.S. marshals, riding for one Federal court or other, were about the only white lawmen a Creek was likely to see in his own country. Concannon shook his head. "Used to be, but not any more. I work for the railroad. I'm lookin' for the men that robbed the train."

That sounded a little foolish, considering that for the past twelve hours he had been running *from* the train robbers. But the Indian accepted it politely and with a straight face. Concannon returned to the time when Turk and Croy had tried to bushwhack him, and did his best

95

to explain how two white men came to be trying to kill a third white man, and what he was doing in Creek country in the first place. "Do you know where Deep Fork is?"

The farmer pointed to the north. "Half a day, maybe. Horseback."

"The trouble is," Concannon confessed, "I don't have a horse. I'd be much obliged if you'd loan me a saddle animal long enough to get to Deep Fork. How much of a town is it?"

The Creek wagged his head from side to side. So-so. Probably about the size of the settlement that Concannon had passed earlier. "Do you know if it's got a wagon yard?"

"Yes."

"I haven't got any money to speak of with me, but a wagon-yard owner would most likely take a draft on the railroad. I could pay you for the use of the animal, if you could see your way clear."

"Why do you go to Deep Fork?"

"I hope to locate a man by the name of Otto Myer and see if he can tell me anything about a well shooter called Ab Miller."

The Indian looked blank. He probably knew that oil prospectors were swarming over his country, sniffing excitedly at ponds where black scum floated on the water, but there was no reason why he should have heard the words "well shooter." Patiently, Concannon explained.

But in the end it wasn't Concannon's patience or his

willingness to explain that made up the Indian's mind. It was the farmer's still, cold hatred of Turk and Croy. Concannon guessed that Turk had made some particularly ugly remark about the farmer's wife, but he wisely decided not to probe too deeply into that. "Wait here," he said to Concannon. Then, tucking his shotgun under his arm, he returned to the house.

Concannon waited.

The farmer came out of the house carrying two drab trade blankets and a length of rope. He waved Concannon toward the barn. "I know short way to Deep Fork. I go with you."

CHAPTER 6

In slightly less than four hours they had raised the settlement of Deep Fork. By that time Concannon was more than ready to end the journey. The life of a railroad agent had not prepared him for four hours aboard a bony mule, a hackamore for a bridle and a threadbare trade blanket for a saddle.

"Wagon yard," the Creek said, pointing to a ramshackle building at the end of the shotgun street. Concannon was surprised at the size of the place; it was more than twice the size of the settlement that he had seen the night before.

"Much obliged," Concannon said, gratefully sliding off the hard-ridged back of the mule. "If you don't mind waitin', I'll see if the railroad's name is worth any money at one of the stores."

The farmer shook his head angrily. "No money!" He was clearly a man who could hate hard and for long stretches at a time. "You kill them two men?"

"I'm hopin' somethin' can be worked out without killin'."

The Indian scowled. He was beginning not to think much of Concannon's courage. With an angry huff he hauled the mule around and, leading Concannon's reluctant animal, rode back into a stand of timber.

Concannon stood for some time looking at a small building next to the wagon yard. There was a sign painted on the side in new black paint. *WELLS DRILLED. FRESH WATER, SALT WATER, PETROLEUM.* OTTO MYER, PROP. In front of the building stood a heavy-duty Studebaker wagon loaded with cable tools.

It took some time for Concannon to convince himself that there actually was such a person as Otto Myer and that he might actually be able to tell him something useful about Ab Miller. So much had happened in the past twenty-four hours that he had come to suspect everything and everyone having anything to do with Miller.

Concannon walked into the building and entered a cloud of smoke and acrid gasses that swirled from a blacksmith's forge in the rear. Raising his voice over the clamor of hammer-on-anvil, Concannon hollered, "Otto Myer?"

The hammering stopped. A small, muscular man, stripped to the waist, turned and squinted at his visitor.

"Hold on a minute. I got to finish this bit while she's hot!"

He worked steadily for several minutes, carefully edging and tempering the heavy drill bit. When he finished he kicked open the back door and let the cold draft clear the building. "You lookin' for a well digger?"

"I'm lookin' for Otto Myer."

"That's me. Best cable tool man in the Creek Nation, if I do say so myself." He laughed explosively but without much humor. "The *only* one. You lookin' for water or oil?"

"Neither one. I want to ask you about a man that used to work for you. Ab Miller. My name's Concannon."

The oilman's gaze sharpened as he looked at Concannon. Then he wheeled, returned to the rear of the building and closed the door. "Ab Miller. What's he done? Blowed hisself up? I always told him he'd do it someday."

"Not that I know of. I just want to find him."

"Why?"

"It's a business matter."

Otto Myer picked up a drill bit as heavy as himself and lugged it to a work bench. "Business with Ab Miller. You don't look like an oilman."

"I'm not."

Myer bent over the bit and inspected the fishtail cutting edge. "Well, it's been six, seven weeks since I seen Ab. I had him shoot a well for me up in the Cherokee country. It didn't work. The hole was too deep and they ain't got anything but shallow stuff up there. The big play's goin' to be here amongst the Creeks—mind what I tell you."

"What happened to Miller after he did the job for you?"

"Lit out, like I just said. He's a nitro man by trade, but wildcattin's in his blood. Like mine. Lord knows where he's at now." He turned and scratched his jaw thoughtfully. "Might be that I could find out where he went to. If you ain't in any hurry."

"I'll be glad to wait, Mr. Myer. I'd be grateful for anything you can find out." It seemed to Concannon that he was always thanking somebody for something, and all it had got him so far was a fine collection of bruises. "Is there a place in Deep Fork that a man could get somethin' to eat?"

"The Fandango, next to the last house on the street, if you don't mind fat meat and cornbread in one form or another. Take your time. Give our little city the once over." He laughed again in his unmirthful way. "I'll let you know soon's as I find out somethin'."

The Fandango was one of those places that spring up in Indian country whenever white men took an interest in it. Up front there was a woodburning cookstove, a counter, and an Indian cook. In the back there were three poker tables and a faro layout. Whiskey was served in china mugs out of a coffeepot.

Concannon took a seat at the counter and asked for eggs, biscuits, fried steak, and molasses. What he got was a bowl of thick corn gruel with pieces of stringy beef floating in it. A woman who was probably in her middle twenties but looked fifty, wearing red stockings and a soiled red velvet dance-hall dress, sat heavily on a stool next to Concannon. She smiled at him wearily, showing twin rows of rotting teeth.

Concannon said, "Sorry, ma'am, I've got just about enough money to pay for this meal."

She shrugged. "It don't matter. It's the slack time of the day and I feel like talkin'." She motioned to the cook. "Here, Chief, pour us a couple of drinks out of the pot." She smiled again at Concannon. "You can afford a couple of whiskies, can't you?"

Concannon decided that he'd rather buy the drinks than argue. The Indian, who obviously disliked being called "Chief," sullenly poured the whiskey and collected the money. Concannon counted his change—it came to a little over two dollars in silver and a five-dollar greenback. When he left Oklahoma City he had forgotten to supply himself with cash. That was what came of traveling so long at railroad expense; he had almost forgotten how important real money could be.

The woman studied her benefactor with frank curiosity as she downed her drink.

Concannon said casually, "I'm lookin' for a man; maybe you know him. Ab Miller. He's a well shooter."

She snorted at the mention of the name. "I know Ab Miller all right. The pal of every dance-hall girl between here and Pennsylvania . . . if it don't cost him any money."

Concannon looked at her with interest. "You happen

to know where I could find him?"

"Miller?" She shook her head and spat on the Fandango's already filthy floor. "I ain't seen him in a month or longer. Wherever he is you can bet he's got hisself a fancy woman makin' his board and room for him."

Without quite knowing why he did it, Concannon lowered his voice. "Do you happen to know a woman in Oklahoma City by the name of Maggie Slatter?"

She looked at him in surprise. "Sure, I know Maggie. We was up in the Cherokee country together; that's where she first run into Miller. Hard luck for Maggie. She's crazy about him—and that means hard luck for any woman." Her eyes narrowed. "Where did a gent like you get to know Maggie?"

"In Oklahoma City. I was there lookin' for Miller."

She shrugged. "Well, if anybody knows, Maggie does."

Not now, Concannon thought to himself. Maggie Slatter is beyond knowing anything. Aloud, he asked, "I wonder if you know a couple of Miller's pals. Men called Turk and Croy."

"Mister, you sure do ask a lot of questions. In a place like Deep Fork that can be dangerous. Besides, I've got a sensitive throat. Hard to talk when I'm dry."

Concannon quickly gave her his drink and asked the Indian to pour another round. The woman grinned. "My name's Bella Plott."

Concannon touched his hatbrim gallantly. "Marcus Concannon, ma'am." One thing he had learned from riding with Ray Allard: treat all women with respect, you never know when you'll be needing their help.

"You're a queer duck, Concannon," Bella Plott told him good-naturedly. "You sound like a law but you don't look like one. I can't make up my mind just what you are."

"I work for the Santa Fe. I'm a railroad agent."

She laughed explosively. "Railroad! The only railroad around here's the A & P, and that's at Red Fork."

"I know," Concannon sighed. "You'll just have to take it on faith, Bella, I'm not tryin' to trick you. I really am lookin' for Miller; it's important."

"I won't be gettin' Maggie in any trouble, will I?"

"I promise, Bella. Maggie's already had all the trouble she's goin' to get." He looked at the cook and motioned for two more whiskies.

Bella tipped the cup and drained it in an offhanded, amiable way. For a while she rocked thoughtfully on the counter stool, then she looked at Concannon and shrugged. "I like you, Concannon. Lord knows why. Men are no goddam good, any of them. And Ab Miller's the worst of the lot. Have you talked to Kate?"

Concannon blinked. This was a name that had not come up before. "Who's Kate?"

"Kate Miller, Ab's wife." She shook her head sadly. "Kate used to work here in the Fandango. That was before the baby come, of course. She can't do it any more." She saw the stunned look on Concannon's face. "You're beginnin' to look queer, mister. Is somethin' ailin' you?"

"I want to make sure we're talkin' about the same

man." From his shirt pocket he took out the tiny tintype picture that he had forgotten to return to Bone. "Is this the Ab Miller that's got a wife here in Deep Fork?"

Bella glanced at the picture and sniffed. "That's Ab Miller. And it'll be a fine, cool day in Hell when you find a more no-account bastard than him."

Concannon stared at the picture, trying to discover what it was about Miller that women found so irresistible. Whatever it was, the photographer had not captured it with his camera. "Could you tell me where this woman—Mrs. Miller—is livin' now?"

"Her shack's just in back of Otto Myer's place. You could almost spit on it from there if the wind was right."

Concannon was getting an uneasy feeling in the pit of his stomach. He left his last greenback on the counter and stood up. "Much obliged for your help, Bella."

"No need to thank me for that," she said, reaching for his untouched whiskey. As Concannon was leaving the Fandango, Bella was tucking the five-dollar bill into the bosom of her dress and preparing herself for a fight with the cook.

Kate Miller's shack was a one-room boxboard shanty sitting on a rocky slope behind Otto Myer's tool shop. Concannon had seen hundreds of places just like it, in mining towns, at end-of-track boomtowns, or any other place where lonely men and desperate women congregated. Kate answered Concannon's knock in her working garb, a sleazy pink slip.

She looked at him wearily, without actually seeing

him. "You'll have to come back later," she said. "The baby's ailin' now." Somewhere in the musty interior of the shack a baby cried.

"I've come about somethin' else, ma'am," Concannon told her. "Do you mind if I ask you about your husband?"

"Ab?" Her hands fluttered to her mouth. "Is somethin' wrong? Was there an accident?"

"No ma'am," Concannon assured her quickly. "I'm tryin' to locate him on a business matter. If you know where I could . . ."

She was already shaking her head. "Ab ain't here. He left. I don't know where he's at."

"I was hopin' you'd heard from him."

Kate Miller almost smiled at the idea of her husband writing a letter. But the baby began crying again and she began closing the door. "No, I ain't heard. Ab never bothers to write."

"Maybe he's got friends," Concannon said quickly when the door was almost closed. "Somebody that might be able to help me."

"No," she said with infinite weariness. "No friends. Nobody." The baby screamed. She closed the door.

Well, Concannon thought philosophically, it was worth a try. He went back to Otto Myer's tool shop, but the oilman was not there.

Concannon's sense of uneasiness began to rise. He had known the feeling before; every lawman had, at one time or another. The cold breath of disaster touched the back of his neck. The cramp of anxiety was in his guts. What

I need, he thought, is a good rifle, a good horse, and a first-class lawman, like Ray Allard, to pard with.

He found himself standing in the middle of Myer's tool shop—just standing there, his mind blank, his eyes staring blindly. He had slipped into a state of half sleep. In another minute or so he would have fallen over. He tried to remember the last time he had stretched out comfortably in bed and slept. He couldn't remember. "I'm not the hoss I used to be," he heard himself announcing to the empty building. "This is young man's work. I ought to get into another business."

He went to Otto Myer's trough of scummy, iron-smelling water, and splashed some of it on his face. He sat down on a nail keg next to the cooling forge and tried to do some thinking about Myer. As if by magic, his thoughts flew back to Oklahoma City. There he was again with Athena Allard. Her grave, unsmiling face filled his mind. For a little while he felt young again, capable of innocent excitement and catfish thoughts which, in other times, would have caused him to burn with embarrassment. Then, after a time, the fog of exhaustion rolled in and there was only darkness and silence.

Time passed. Minutes or hours, Concannon didn't know. As if from a great distance he heard a burst of harsh, unpleasant laughter.

"Come alive, Concannon. We got us a little business to attend to. Settlin'-up day is at hand."

Groggily, Concannon opened his eyes. He had fallen forward on the keg, bent almost double. His back was stiff, his mouth dry. His head felt stuffed with cotton batting. A big hand grasped his shoulder and jerked him upright. Concannon stared into the savagely grinning face of the red-haired Turk.

Instinctively, Concannon grabbed for his .38. But the holster was empty. And the big .45 was no longer in his waistband.

Croy was standing beside his partner scratching himself and looking bored. "Won't be long till sundown," he said to Otto Myer. "There ain't nothin' much we can do before then, except set steady"

Turk raised his rifle, placed the cold muzzle against Concannon's forehead and smiled. "I don't feel much like waitin'. I'm goin' to kill him."

"Later," Croy told him patiently. "We got to wait till dark; then we'll get him out of town. Then you can kill him."

Otto Myer was scowling at the three of them. "I don't like the notion of keepin' him here in the tool shop."

"Just till dark," Croy assured him. "Then we'll take him away and you'll be out of it."

Turk spat viciously and pressed the muzzle harder against Concannon's forehead. "I say kill him now."

"No!" Myer said in alarm. "I don't want the blood. I don't want deputy U.S. marshals sniffin' around. Take him off somewheres if you got to kill him."

"He's right," Croy told his partner. "Folks here've got a nice quiet little town. What would they think if we went and stirred things up and got the gover'ment marshals mad? There'd be hell to pay all around, and we don't want that."

Turk's expression didn't change. "Yes, sir," he said as though he hadn't heard anything they had said, "I say kill him now and get it over with."

For a moment Croy looked mildly irritated. "You go and make a fuss—what do you think *he's* goin' to say about that?"

For a moment Turk stood perfectly still, his finger hard on the trigger. Concannon didn't move. He didn't breathe. Even his heart seemed to stop beating. Then, very slowly, the outlaw took the muzzle away from Concannon's head. "Later," he grinned, flashing his yellow teeth. "I'll be thinkin' about it, Concannon." Suddenly he laughed. "*You* can be thinkin' about it."

"No fuss, no shootin', no blood!" Otto Myer was saying excitedly. "That was the bargain we had!"

"That's the bargain you'll get," Croy assured him. "You got a piece of rope we can use?"

They tied Concannon's feet and hands and casually dumped him on the ground next to the forge. "Stuff a rag in his mouth, in case he takes it in his head to holler," Croy said. "And lock the doors. You're closed for business, Myer, until we're away from here."

With pleasure, Turk stuffed a sooty rag into Concannon's mouth. Then he hunkered down so that he could see the fear in Concannon's eyes. "How you like that, railroad agent? You ought to of listened to reason back at Oklahoma City when we talked to you. But your kind never listens, do you?"

"Leave him alone," Croy said with a touch of weariness. "You can have your fun later."

"Later! Always later!" Turk snarled. "It's always the same, you and *him* alike!"

Croy looked sharply at his partner. His voice was angry. "Shut up, you talk too much."

"What difference does it make? It ain't goin' to make any difference to *him*. He glared at Concannon.

"Just forget about it. When this little job's over and we get the money . . ." Croy shrugged. "Then you can do whatever comes in your head."

Now it was beginning to take shape in Concannon's mind. He closed his eyes and shut out Turk's viciously grinning face. He shut out the voices and the smells and the sounds. He made himself be quiet and calm as he studied the pieces of the puzzle.

It was clear now that Turk and Croy had got to Deep Fork ahead of Concannon. So they must have known ahead of time where he was headed. More than that, they had known that he was going to talk to Myer. So they got to Myer first and bought his cooperation. The question now was how had they known? Who could have told them?

That part of the puzzle would have to be fitted together later. He opened his eyes and saw that Turk was now standing at the small window in the front part of the building, sullenly glaring out at the town. Croy was simply standing near the tool dressing bench looking into space. Otto Myer was pacing nervously.

"Mister," the little oilman said to Concannon, "I sure never aimed for it to work out like this. I never figgered they aimed to *kill* you."

Croy turned and looked at him blankly but said nothing.

"They said they just wanted to talk to you. On business," Myer went on uncomfortably. "Well, I needed the money. Wildcatters always need money. It didn't sound like anything bad, the way they told it"

"Shut up," Croy told him absently, in a tone that said he didn't really care one way or the other.

"How come ever'body's so interested in Ab Miller all of a sudden?" the oilman asked in a whining tone.

"Less you know, longer you'll live," Croy told him.

Myer looked shocked. He started to say something, then changed his mind. He shrugged and paced in aimless circles. The sun was less than thirty minutes high.

After a while Turk turned away from the window and came back to where Concannon lay. "Won't be long now, Concannon. If you're a prayin' man, now's the time to get started."

Darkness settled like a soft black fog on the wooded hills. At last Croy said, "Myer, go out for a look-see. If ever'thing's quiet, bring up the horses."

The oilman slipped out the back door. Within a few minutes he was back. "Ever'thing's quiet. Except the Fandango. I got the horses tied up in the alley."

Turk drew a skinning knife out of his belt and hunkered down beside Concannon. "You got your prayin' done, railroad man?" He put the point of the knife to Concannon's throat and Concannon flinched. Turk chuckled. Then he cut the ropes that bound Concannon's ankles and hands.

Croy came up and helped pull Concannon to his feet. "No monkeyshines now. Ever'thing quiet and easy."

Outside three horses were waiting. The two outlaws boosted Concannon to the saddle. Otto Myer stood in the doorway of his tool shop, his face glistening with sweat. On that chill autumn night, with a foretaste of winter in the air, the little oilman was sweating freely. Concannon thought about that for a minute. He scarcely noticed that Turk was cursing angrily under his breath and tying his hands to the saddle horn. There was something about that little wildcatter . . .

Myer wiped his moist forehead on his sleeve and sidled toward Concannon. "Mister," he said, quietly stroking the animal's withers, "I never aimed for it to wind up the way it has. It ain't my fault. I want you to believe that."

A voice in the back of Concannon's mind asked quietly, "What's the matter with him? In a few minutes I'll be dead, and he'll be out of danger. And he'll have his money that he got from Turk and Croy. What's he so sweaty about?" Aloud he said nothing.

Myer shot a nervous look at the two outlaws. "I'd rest easier in my mind," he told Concannon, "if you'd just nod your head or somethin', to let me know that you don't hold me to blame for any of this"

Turk snorted in disgust. "You gutless wonders make me sick!"

The little wildcatter didn't appear to hear him. He stared up at Concannon, anxiously waiting for his nod of absolution. The voice in Concannon's mind was still asking, "What's ailin' him?" At last, grudgingly, he nodded.

The little oilman sighed deeply with relief. Then, as Turk and Croy were climbing into their saddles, he moved close to Concannon's animal and spoke quickly, under his breath. "The bend in the road. North of town."

Concannon stared down at him, waiting for something else, but Otto Myer stepped quickly away and ducked into his tool shop and closed the door. The bend in the road. North of town. That was all.

Croy and Turk, now mounted, moved in on either side of Concannon. "Nice and easy. No fuss or racket." Turk grinned, his yellow teeth flashing in the darkness. Expertly, the two outlaws hazed Concannon away from the tool shop and onto the rutted wagon track that passed as a road.

Concannon's mind was racing in circles. His hands, lashed tightly to the saddle horn, were numb. There was an ache in his guts. What had the wildcatter been trying to tell him?

The darkness was soft and smoky, the darkness of early evening. A prickling sensation, like the sting of nettles, raced across Concannon's scalp. There it was, the bend in the road, less than five minutes north of Deep Fork. They were riding quietly, three abreast, toward a stand of dark timber. There was nothing there that Concannon could see. Only the timber.

As they rode beneath an umbrella of towering cottonwoods, Turk and Croy bore in on either side of Concannon.

Now they were well into the bend that Otto Myer warned him about. Nothing happened. It was just a bend in the wagon track, following the meandering of a wooded stream. As the darkness became deeper the ache in Concannon's guts became more painful. If anything was going to happen, this is where it would be. Cautiously, he slipped his boots out of the stirrups. Suddenly he kicked out with both feet, slamming the toes of his boots into the animals that bore in on either side of him.

Startled, the horses grunted and reared high, pawing the air. A volley of rifle fire shattered the night. The frightened animals bolted.

Concannon lay low over his animal's neck and tried to knee in toward the timber. A big hand reached out of the night, took the horse's headstall and skillfully guided it behind a wall of black-green vines. A short distance upstream there was fitful firing of rifles.

"Be quiet," a deep, calm voice told Concannon. "Light Horse here. Everything all right."

Concannon stared at the brown, almost invisible face of the other horseman. It was the Creek farmer who had brought him to Deep Fork that morning. Unhurriedly, the Indian freed Concannon of his gag and cut the ropes from his wrists. Concannon rubbed his numb hands together. His tongue felt too big for his mouth. As soon as he could speak he said, "How many Light Horse are there?"

"Two," the Creek told him.

"Where did they come from? Where did *you* come from? I thought you went back to your farm."

The Indian shrugged. In spare, slow English, he explained that he had not gone to the farm but to the Indian police. He had returned to Deep Fork with the two Light Horsemen. That, for the moment, was all Concannon got to hear.

Somewhere upstream a rifle fired. It had a hesitant sound. A fight with Indian police was the one thing that Croy and Turk hadn't bargained for.

There were several moments of strained silence. Apparently the outlaws had dismounted to face the attack from the Indians. Now, both outlaws and Indians seemed to be thoughtfully considering the situation. Concannon, in spite of the farmer's explanation, was still puzzled. For one thing, the Indian police were usually careful to stay out of the affairs of the white intruder; that was a job for Federal deputy marshals. "Don't think I'm not grateful for what you did," Concannon said. "You saved my hide. But how did you get the Light Horse to interfere?"

The Indian shrugged. "Told them you Indian."

Concannon digested this slowly. For an Indian to lie to a Light Horse policeman was a serious matter.

"The man you call Turk," the farmer explained. "He speak bad words to my woman." That, as far as he was concerned, explained everything.

"What will you do when they find out I'm not Indian and they've been interfering with Federal law?"

The farmer did not look as if he cared much about Federal law. But he did care about the Light Horse, and he was beginning to think he'd better not be on hand when they learned that he had tricked them. He sat for a moment, looking at Concannon. Then he unslung the long-barreled shotgun that he had been carrying across his shoulders. "Sometime you give this to Indian agent. I get it from him."

Concannon was startled by the gesture. An Indian did not lightly hand over his personal weapon, least of all a Creek, and to a white man at that. Concannon accepted the weapon and a handful of shells as if they were pure gold. "I don't even know your name."

"Bruce McFarland," the Indian said.

Concannon stared at him but was careful not to laugh or even smile. A man with a name like Marcus Concannon soon learned that a person's name was no joking matter. "I'll give it to the agent. Much obliged, Mr. McFarland."

The Indian raised his hand in a curiously formal gesture of farewell. Then he reined his mule around and quietly melted into the dark timber.

CHAPTER 7

Croy and Turk lay behind a fallen cottonwood, a few feet from the water. Turk was in a cold and savage rage. The two outlaws still didn't know what happened, just that Concannon had spooked their horses and then the unexpected rifle fire had sent the animals into a panic. Now they were afoot, with only one rifle between them. As he had fallen from his horse, Turk had not been able to rescue his saddle gun. Besides that, he had painfully twisted his knee in the spill, which did nothing to improve his short-fused temper.

A night breeze rattled the cottonwood leaves. Turk had Croy's .45 in his hand, pointing it at the darkness. "How many was there, you think?"

"Hard to tell. Two, maybe. Two rifles."

"Who are they? Where'd they come from?"

Croy shrugged. "Deputy marshals, maybe. We'll know before long"

"How?"

"If they set their teeth in us," Croy said dryly, "and hang on till we're finished, then we'll know they're deputy marshals."

Turk snorted angrily. After a minute he asked, "How you figger they got on to us, whoever they are?"

"Myer. He's the only one that knowed."

Turk's eyes seemed to glitter. "I'll know what to do about Myer next time I see him again."

"Of course,' Croy went on calmly, "it may not be the marshals at all. Recollect the Indian that you tangled with this mornin'? Myer claimed it was an Indian that brought Concannon to Deep Fork—might be he was sore enough to turn the Light Horse on us."

This was a possibility that Turk had not thought about before. In anger and frustration, he thought about it now. "Then where's Concannon now?"

"Don't worry about Concannon. He hasn't got a gun; we'll find him sooner or later."

"Or them two sharpshooters don't find us first," Turk said bitterly.

Croy was working on an idea. He turned it quietly in his mind, studying it from all angles. "The more I think about it," he said finally, "the more I think they might be Light Horse. I keep rememberin' the look of that Indian farmer. He was mad enough to pull a stunt like this. He'll have hell to pay later, when the Indian police figger out he tricked them. But that don't matter now."

"Whoever they are, we can't set here jawin' all night. We've got to find them and kill them."

Croy looked at his partner and said dryly, "I expected that was about what you'd figger. But we can save the killin' till later, if it comes to that." Suddenly he raised his voice and called to the night. "You boys hear me out there? You lissen good if you do, because I ain't goin' to say this but once!"

There was a moment of nervous rustling downstream. Then silence.

Croy hollered, "If you're Indians, or Indian police, you're about to get yourselves in a mess of trouble. We're white men here. We was mindin' our own business till you come along and bushwhacked us." He gave them a few seconds to think. Then he went on. "Unless you fellers aim to start a war with the gover'ment marshals you'd be smart to light out of here and let us white folks take care of our own business."

There was a sound of movement from downstream. "They're talkin' it over," Croy said, drawing a deep breath of relief. "They're Indians, all right."

They listened hard as the two riflemen dropped their caution and began a rapid-fire argument in Creek. A slow smile spread over Turk's face. "By God, that's redstick talk, sure enough!"

The talk stopped. An uneasy and angry decision had been reached. Turk and Croy lay smiling behind their cottonwood breastworks, listening to the two Light Horse making their way downstream. The Indians were pulling out. Then they heard the sound of horses heading cross-country. "I wouldn't want to be that Creek farmer, when they catch him," Turk grinned. Then the grin vanished and his voice was harsh. "And I wouldn't want to be Concannon, when I catch *him*."

Concannon listened to the sound of the retreating Indian policemen. He could expect no more miracles. No more enraged farmers to bail him out of trouble. But he did have a choke-barrel shotgun and a dozen rounds of buckshot, which Turk and Croy didn't know about.

Croy called, "You hear me, Concannon? We're right back where we started, looks like. Just the three of us out to settle our little differences amongst ourselves." He sounded calm and relaxed and pleased with himself. Concannon could almost see him scratching himself and gazing idly up at the night sky. "Up to now you been playin' in luck, Concannon. But luck, like ever'thing else, comes to an end sometime. This here's the time for you, looks like.

It was just talk, something he hoped to hold Concannon's attention while Turk changed positions.

Concannon tucked the shotgun under his arm and began squirming through the brush. He tried not to think of Turk who might be taking a position on the upper bank at this moment. A snapping twig sounded like a pistol shot in his ear. He lay for a long while, his heart pounding, his mouth dry.

Croy had stopped talking now. A vagrant breeze drifted through the creek bottom and cottonwood branches rattled like bones. Concannon wiped his forehead on his sleeve and continued his squirming way upstream.

A thin sliver of brilliant orange appeared above the opposite creekbank. Concannon watched it, appalled, as a great, red October moon rose up behind the trees. In his eyes the moon seemed unbelievably bright, sending dazzling ripples shooting along the water, lighting the sky. Concannon lay in a sparse stand of weeds and felt suddenly naked. It didn't seem possible that Turk and Croy could fail to see him.

A sudden recklessness took hold of him. He reminded himself that his string of luck had run out; from here on out he would have to make his own luck. With that thought in mind, he lurched upright in the weed patch and threw himself down the sandy bank toward the water.

A rifle roared. Concannon braced himself for an instant, aimed at the muzzle flash and fired the shotgun. The kick against his shoulder knocked him off balance; he fell and rolled several times without knowing whether the shot had been effective. But in a relatively calm and orderly chamber of his mind he realized that the rifle was no longer firing. From somewhere a pistol fired rapidly three times. It paused for a moment and fired twice more.

Concannon was puzzled. Why would a killer use a pistol if he could get his hands on a rifle? The answer was that one of the outlaws had lost his rifle.

Now the night, red with moonlight, was silent again. Quickly Concannon fumbled in his pocket, found a shell and shoved it into the breech of the shotgun. On the upper bank he could hear one of the killers hurriedly reloading his revolver.

But what about the rifleman? Was he dead or playing possum? Was it Turk or was it Croy?

Concannon crawled into a patch of dry weeds and lay still. The gunman on the upper bank had finished reloading and was beginning to edge in toward the water. That would be Turk. Too impatient and enraged to play a waiting game. For a few seconds Concannon felt almost sorry for Turk. Hand gun against buckshot, it really wasn't much of a contest now.

The moon rose higher in the gunmetal sky. Concannon stared at it in fascination. It seemed to float just above the still stream, making the water a shining ribbon.

Turk fired again with the pistol. Concannon reacted automatically by pointing the shotgun at the muzzle flash and pulling the trigger. He saw a blurred figure reel back into the brush. Something small and heavy hit the ground. The pistol.

Then all was still.

The yellow cottonwood leaves glittered like gold dollars in the moonlight. Concannon lay perfectly motionless, pressed to the ground. He lay that way until his leg began to cramp. Then he put another shell in the shotgun and began making his way cautiously up the bank.

Croy lay behind the bone-white trunk of the fallen cottonwood. He lay face-up with his arms outspread, as if appealing to the Almighty to correct this injustice that had overtaken him. Most of his face was missing. Concannon recognized him by his clothing; otherwise he couldn't have been sure which of the outlaws he had killed.

Concannon placed Croy's hat over what was left of his face and again began inching his way up the bank. In life Croy had not been an especially pleasant person to look at; in death he was much worse. Concannon blanked that out of his mind and concentrated on Turk.

He pulled up a short distance from where he had last seen the falling outlaw. "Are you there, Turk?" Concannon murmured bleakly. "Are you dead? Or are you lurkin' in those black weeds like an old wounded cougar, waitin' for me to come into point-blank pistol range?"

Turk didn't say.

The night sighed. The moon, as though it had suddenly become bored with the violence, continued on its way across the still sky. Concannon lay where he was, staring at the brush and sweating. After what seemed a very long time, the outlaw groaned.

". . . Concannon . . . Help me."

Concannon gripped the shotgun until the muscles in

his forearm began to jump. "If I had the sense of a spotted horse," he said to himself coldly, "I'd end it here and now. One more shot, right into the middle of the brush. That would finish it."

"Concannon . . . goddam you, you killed me!"

It was not much more than a whisper, the last thread of a life that was rapidly unraveling. Concannon brought the shotgun to his shoulder and aimed at the brush.

Then he lowered the weapon and continued his way through the weeds.

Turk was lying back on one elbow, his eyes burning in rage, his chest crimson. His pistol lay on the ground about six feet away, but he could not reach it. Concannon quickly got to his feet and grabbed the revolver.

As Turk cursed him feebly, Concannon went down on one knee and inspected the wound. There was nothing to be done for him. Only his hate had kept Turk alive this long. "It's not so bad," Concannon told him calmly. "I'll go back to Deep Fork in a minute and see if I can locate a doc."

Turk's supporting arm collapsed and he fell back with his head in the weeds. Concannon propped him up a little, put his hat under his head and went through the motions of attending to the wound. "You want to tell me about it, Turk? About the robbery? Ab Miller? It'll make it easier on you later, when your case comes to trial."

". . . You're a rotten liar, Concannon. I won't live to see no trial, and we both know it."

"You can't tell about that. I've seen plenty of horses get well after the vet said to shoot them." He tore off part of the outlaw's shirt and formed a bandage and pressed it over the gaping hole in his chest. "Tell me," he said casually, "who was behind it all? Who thought up the robbery? Miller?"

Turk called him an obscene name and fell to coughing. There were bloody bubbles at the corner of his mouth; Concannon wiped them away.

"Where is Miller? That money's not goin' to do you any good now. But it might help you in court later, if you talk to me."

". . . Go to hell, Concannon."

"Well, just to ease my curiosity then. Why are you and Croy and Miller still hangin' out in the Territory, with half the officers in the Federal courts lookin' for you?"

Turk summoned strength for one last savage grin. "You'd like to know, wouldn't you?"

"Yes. I could help you, Turk. You'd have the railroad behind you, if you helped get that money back."

The outlaw groaned and muttered another obscenity. "Why didn't you kill me that night in Oklahoma City, Turk, instead of just stoving in a few ribs?"

The fire of hatred was flickering. He stared at Concannon blankly.

"Tell me just one thing, Turk. Why did you threaten Ray Allard's widow and then try to bribe her with two thousand dollars?"

A crimson froth bubbled at Turk's mouth—in the moonlight it was almost black. He looked at Concannon as if he were enjoying some secret joke all his own. Then the fire went out.

Concannon climbed the bank to the wagon track and walked back to Deep Fork. It was not much of a walk; ten minutes at most. To him it seemed as long as the stage road from Dodge to Denver. He was panting when he got to the Fandango. His clothing was in tatters, his pants out at the knees, his hands bloody. There was a sudden and stunned silence when he walked into the illegal saloon.

He stood in the doorway, a Creek farmer's shotgun in his hand, an outlaw's .45 in his waistband, a disturbing blend of rage and exhaustion in his face.

A poker game came to an abrupt halt in middeal. The faro players pocketed their money. For a moment the only sound in the place was the Indian cook's heavy breathing.

Then Bella Plott left her stool at the counter and came toward him shaking her head. "Mister, you sure are full of surprises."

"I want to see Otto Myer."

Without taking her eyes off Concannon's face, she bellowed, "Otto, a gent to see you!"

The little oilman, with one of the Fandango's girls on his arm, appeared from behind a gingham curtain in the back of the place. His face went white when he saw Concannon.

"I don't guess anybody heard the shootin' a while back," Concannon said, looking at Myer. "There was plenty of it, and not far off. There've been wars won and lost with less shootin'. But I guess nobody heard."

He realized that he was slightly lightheaded and not

making much sense. Bella Plott continued to stare at him, wagging her head gravely. "Nobody heard a thing here, mister. Not a thing."

"And I don't guess anybody saw a couple of strangers ride into town today around dinnertime. A little before I got here."

"No sir. Nobody seen nothin'."

Otto Myer was moving slowly toward Concannon as if he were being reeled in on a string. "No trouble here, Concannon. You know the kind of place it is."

"I know. By this time tomorrow it's goin' to be full of United States deputy marshals if somebody's memory doesn't start to improve."

The poker players folded their hands and started toward the back door. The faro players were just behind them.

"All right," the little wildcatter sighed, licking his dry lips. "We'll go over to the tool shop, that's the best place."

"Where's the nearest deputy marshal? Red Fork?" Reluctantly, Otto Myer nodded. "I guess."

"Send somebody to get him."

Bella Plott stared at him in alarm. "You can't do that! A liquor house in Indian country, they'd tear my place down plank by plank!"

"You'll have all night to get rid of your whiskey. I want to talk to the marshal tomorrow mornin'."

Concannon and the nervous wildcatter left the Fandango and went to the tool shop. "Mister," Myer said worriedly, "you sure take some chances. Bella runs a quiet place; she's never had it raided."

"I don't want to talk about Bella right now. I want to talk about Ab Miller." He sat on the keg next to the forge, holding the shotgun across his knees.

Myer turned up the coal oil lamp and groaned to himself. "I wish I'd never heard of Ab Miller. He's a well shooter, that's all I know about him. Used to be the best there is, but lately he's been gettin' nervous. Nitro men don't last long after that, when they start gettin' nervous."

"His trade was beginnin' to scare him." That's what Maggie Slatter had said. Ab Miller had bad dreams; he wanted enough money to get into another business. "How long did you know Miller?"

"Three, four years, off and on."

"How well did you know Turk and Croy?"

The wildcatter looked blank. Concannon added, "The two gents that paid you to set me up for murder."

"I never seen that pair before, and that's the Lord's truth!" He wiped a nervous hand across his mouth. "You don't really want to talk to a deputy marshal, do you?"

"First thing tomorrow mornin'. Now tell me how you knew the Light Horse would be there waitin' for us tonight?"

Myer looked at him pleadingly, then shrugged in resignation. "While them two hardcases was holdin' you here in the tool shop word got out that two Indian policemen was sniffin' around. An Indian farmer by the name of McFarland had made a complaint and brought in the Light Horse. Well, you know how it is. Can't

126

afford to have police, even if they're Indians, sniffin' around a place like this. So I located the farmer and made a deal with him. I'd tell him how to ambush the two hardcases if he'd keep the Light Horse out of Deep Fork."

"Makin' deals is your line," Concannon said dryly. "Where are the Light Horse now?"

"Lit out. Nothin' in it for Indians, messin' in white folks' business."

"That's why I want the deputy marshal in the mornin'. Now," Concannon said, with every muscle aching, "I'm goin' to get some sleep."

He slept fitfully on a folded tarp in Myer's tool shop. In his dreams he saw Ray and Athena Allard, and both of them were laughing. This was the strangest part of the dream—awake he had never seen Athena laugh.

He awoke at dawn. Otto Myer unlocked the front door to the tool shop and came toward Concannon with a tall lawman at his side. "This here's Deputy Marshal Harry Wingate," the little oilman said to Concannon. "He's stationed at Red Fork."

Myer left them alone and Concannon told the marshal about the fight and what he knew about the two outlaws. Everything was crisp and businesslike; the routine was thoroughly familiar to both of them. Concannon made a brief statement in writing and signed it. "I guess you'll want to see the bodies."

Wingate nodded. "Then you can go. If we need you we can get you through the railroad."

"I'd be obliged to you," Concannon told him, "if there wasn't any trouble made for the two Light Horsemen or the fanner. They saved my hide. I guess it wasn't what they had in mind last night, but they saved it all the same."

The marshal grinned and shrugged. "It's not the Indians that make work for us. Ridin' into town I saw a place, the Fandango. What kind of place is it?"

"A blind pig, like any other place in a town like this. Bella Plott is the owner. She's most likely got rid of her whiskey by this time, though."

Wingate smiled bleakly. "Well, let's go look at your two friends."

Turk and Croy looked even deader by daylight than they had by moonlight. The marshal removed the hat from Croy's face and grunted with distaste. A careful worker, Wingate searched the bodies and listed everything he found. Pocket knives, tobacco, cheap nickel-plated watches. Less than ten dollars in cash between them.

"You sure these men had a hand in that train robbery?"

Concannon sighed. "It's the best guess I can make. Maybe I'm wrong."

"Well . . ." They stood there for a while breathing in the brisk autumn air and making a point of not looking at the dead men. Wingate still had a lot of work ahead of him, writing reports, making inquiries, arranging burials. Death always caused work for a lawman. "How do you like workin' for the railroad?" the marshal asked at last.

"Not bad. I've got a boss that's not the easiest man in the world to get along with. But I guess you have too."

They both smiled. "There are times when I think I could use a change."

"If I can be any help, just let me know. You can always get me through the railroad."

They might have been two businessmen, casual friends meeting on the street or over a whiskey in a familiar saloon. "How do you aim to get back to Oklahoma City?" Wingate asked.

"Rent a saddle animal, I guess. If the railroad's name is any good here."

"The railroad's name is always good." Both men smiled again, as if something clever had been said. On the ground at their feet Turk and Croy got deader and deader.

As they walked back to the road, Concannon said, "There's one favor you can do for me if you don't mind. Hold up your report for a day or so. When I get back to Oklahoma City it might be interestin' to see if anybody's surprised to see I'm still alive."

Wingate nodded comfortably. "I couldn't get my report through to Oklahoma City in less than a week if I tried."

CHAPTER 8

When Concannon entered the Travelers lobby the desk clerk said, "Sergeant Bone has been asking for you, Mr. Concannon."

"Sergeant Bone will have to wait. Is there anything else?"

The clerk was well trained and suited to his calling, but he couldn't help staring at Concannon's tattered clothing and bearded face. "Yes sir," he said, reaching into a pigeonhole, "here's a message for you."

It was a telegram from John Evers in Chicago BOARD MEMBERS INSIST ON SOLUTION TO ROBBERY STOP EXPECT POSITIVE RESULTS WITHOUT DELAY. That was John Evers's way of letting him know that his job was hanging in the balance. "See there's plenty of hot water upstairs," Concannon told the clerk. "I've got some cleanin' up to do."

He bathed until his skin was raw from scrubbing and still he did not feel very clean. He could still see the fire of hatred dying in Turk's eyes, and the mess that had once been Croy's face. All of that, and he still didn't know any more about Ab Miller than he had before, except that he was hell with the ladies, and he was married and had a baby. He wondered if Maggie Slatter had known that.

Pat Duncan, owner of the Fine and Dandy Cafe, greeted Concannon with obvious hostility, but he did not seem especially surprised to see him alive. "Mrs. Allard ain't here," he said in answer to Concannon's question.

"Where is she?"

"She's . . ." The cook lowered his eyes. "She's at the cemetery."

At the cemetery there was a black hearse drawn by matched blacks standing beside an open grave. Several rigs of one kind and another were drawn up along a whitewashed fence. About thirty mourners milled aimlessly about the grave while the pallbearers got the casket out of the hearse.

Concannon spoke to one of the onlookers. "Somebody important must have died."

"They did. The head whore at Nina Truelove's. Got herself killed in a cuttin' scrape and some of her customers chipped in to give her a fancy sendoff."

A lanky preacher in a black clawhammer coat read the service over the casket. The mourners, most of them men, didn't look very interested. They lounged about the open grave, smoking and gazing into the distance, thinking their own thoughts. Probably they had been drunk when the fancy sendoff had been arranged; now it didn't seem like such a good idea.

On the far side of the hearse a vaguely familiar figure stood talking to two gravediggers. Concannon thought for a minute. Lawson was the man's name. Lawson the undertaker. He was quietly chuckling at something one of the gravediggers had just said. Concannon skirted the gathering at the grave and made for the undertaker.

"Mr. Lawson, I'm lookin' for a grave and I don't know where it is. I wonder if you could help me?"

The undertaker sobered immediately. "Concannon, ain't it? You came to my place once with Sergeant Bone. Whose grave are you lookin' for, Mr. Concannon?"

"Ray Allard. The railroad agent that was killed in the train robbery."

The undertaker stared blankly for a moment. Then he

brightened. "I recollect now, it's the new block of lots over there behind the big liveoak tree." He sighed and looked professionally grave. "Sad to-do all around, the Allard funeral. I remember it very well, now that you mention it."

"How do you mean? Was it sadder than the usual run of funerals?"

"I guess that depends on how you look at it. I was speaking professionally. Nobody could of done any better than I did—anybody'll tell you that. But it wasn't very, well, satisfyin'. If you know what I mean. Oh, it was *decent,* mind you. Inexpensive and . . . decent." He didn't like the taste of the word. His mouth puckered in distaste. "I did the best I could, the very best, under the circumstances, but there really ain't much you can do with a closed casket service." He shook his head ruefully as he remembered the unprofitable funeral.

"Much obliged for your help," Concannon said dryly. He walked off leaving the undertaker still shaking his head.

He saw her standing on the tawny slope just beyond the liveoak tree. She might have been standing on the moon, she was so completely alone. A small bunch of autumn flowers, yellow chrysanthemums, lay next to the small stone marker. The prairie wind was sighing.

Concannon drew up beneath the liveoak and lit a cigar and waited. Now that he was here he did not quite know why he had come. There was nothing more that she could tell him about Croy or Turk or Ab Miller. Nothing that she could tell him about Ray that he didn't know. He

132

had come simply because he had wanted to see her again.

But he wished that it could have been somewhere else. Even the cafe, or the ice-cream parlor. Anywhere but here. But he didn't go away. He stood there quietly smoking, watching her. She didn't know or care if she was being watched. She merely stood there, beautiful and pale and unapproachable, the only person left in the world. Her world.

Up the slope, near the entrance to the cemetery, the graveside service for the whore was breaking up. The gravediggers were shoveling the red clay back into the hole. The mourners were hurriedly making for their rigs. Within a few minutes the area was cleared—except for that conscientious professional man, Mr. Lawson, and his two helpers.

At last she turned away from the grave and started up the slope. She looked so pale that Concannon was alarmed. He stepped out quickly and said, "Mrs. Allard, are you all right?"

She looked at him blankly. For several seconds she didn't even recognize him. With apparent effort she focused her thoughts and placed him in her mind. "Mr. Concannon," she said at last. "Yes, I am well, thank you."

This is ridiculous, Concannon thought to himself. I can't even call her by her given name, and she doesn't care if I'm alive or dead. Aloud he said, "I have a hack waiting on the other side of the fence; can I take you back to town?"

It was a matter of such small importance that she could only nod. "All right."

They walked in silence to the top of the slope, picking their way between the graves. A big graveyard, Concannon thought, for a town so young. He had the feeling that he ought to say something, about Ray, or his trip to Deep Fork, or the two men he had killed. Something. But all he said was, "Watch out for the rocks; the ground's rough along here."

Concannon handed her into the hack and got in himself. "Do you want to go back to the cafe?" he asked.

She shook her head. "No. To Mrs. Robertson's, if you please."

She didn't ask what had brought him to the cemetery or what he had been doing since she had last seen him. At last, after a long silence, she said, "Mr. Concannon, may I ask a favor of you?"

"Yes ma'am, what is it?"

"I have decided that it's no longer important for me to stay here and clear Ray's name. I no longer care what others think of him. I know what I think of him—that's enough. I want you to stop your investigation."

Concannon stared at her. "Would you mind tellin' me why?"

"I want to forget, that's all. I want to go away and forget."

"Go away?"

She nodded. "Back to my parents' place in Kansas."

Concannon had the uneasy feeling that they were speaking different languages and that neither of them understood a word of what the other had said. "Could you tell me what made you change your mind this way? Three days ago, before I left for Deep Fork, you said the most important thing in the world was seein' that Ray's name was cleared."

"I know. But I was wrong. Don't you understand, Mr. Concannon, all I want is to forget?"

At West Seventh Street the driver turned onto Broadway. "I'm afraid," he said slowly, "that a railroad investigation is more complicated than you've got it figured. If I drop the case somebody else will pick it up. There's no way I can stop it."

Nothing in her face changed. After a moment she said, "You're right, of course. It was foolish of me to ask."

"No ma'am, it wasn't that. I know how you feel; I'll try to keep everything as quiet as possible."

She nodded absently, her mind somewhere else. Concannon asked, "When do you figure to start back to Kansas?"

"I'm not sure. Soon." As the driver braked in front of the Robertson rooming house, she turned to Concannon and looked at him directly for the first time. "I'm afraid I've caused you a lot of trouble, Mr. Concannon."

"No ma'am, not that. Never that."

"I'm sorry," she said. "For everything." She smiled the faintest smile that Concannon had ever seen. Then she was gone.

The driver looked back at Concannon. "You want to go back to town now?"

"The Day and Night, on Bunco Alley," Concannon

told him. He didn't look forward to facing Lily Olse[n] now, but it was time he made a report to Sergeant Bone.

Lily was behind the bar feeding Satan cream and sar[-]dines in a china dish. She looked at Concannon with n[o] particular feeling, as she might have looked at any othe[r] regular customer. "Bone's lookin' for you. He said if yo[u] came in, to wait."

"How'd he know I was back?"

Lily Olsen shrugged. "I don't ask Bone about his busi[-]ness, and he don't ask about mine." Then, "Oh hell," sh[e] said, dropping her act of chill unconcern. "I don't kno[w] what's got into Bone. But he's mad about somethin'. Madder than usual, I mean. Are you in trouble with th[e] police?"

"Not that I know of."

She set up a bottle of Tennessee whiskey and poure[d] him a drink. Concannon downed it and the mellow ol[d] liquor lay warm and comforting in his stomach. H[e] regarded the bottle fondly. He knew very well that th[e] solutions to his problems would not be found at th[e] bottom of a bottle, but the thought was tempting. H[e] carefully measured another drink and downed it.

Lily looked at him with concern; it wasn't in her char[-]acter to hold a grudge or stay angry for long stretches. "Are you all right, Concannon?"

"I'm tired and some the worse for wear, but I'm al[l] right."

"I know it's not the polite thing to do," she said dryly "to say I told you so. But I told you so."

Concannon grinned. "I remember. Will you join me in another round of this excellent Tennessee whiskey?"

"No, thanks, I've got a business to run." She shrugged resignedly. "You can take the bottle upstairs if you want to. I'll be busy down here."

"Lily," Concannon told her with feeling, "you're a wonder."

"You want me to send Bone up, if he comes?"

"Send him up, send him up." He was already a little lightheaded. It had been a busy day and again he had forgotten to eat.

Satan followed Concannon up the stairs on the off chance that he was smuggling in a can of salmon or sardines. The cat bounded onto the needlepoint settee and watched curiously as this tall, familiar figure prowled Lily's sitting room. Concannon poured himself a drink and looked down into those yellow eyes. "Son," he said gravely, "I've just about decided that you're the smartest gent in Oklahoma. Petted and pampered, livin' the life of luxury. First class grub, a soft bed to sleep in. Nobody kickin' in your ribs or tryin' to bushwhack you at every turn."

The cat looked at him and yawned.

Concannon took the bottle to an armchair that was too small for him, but he wedged himself onto it and dozed for a while in a comfortable whiskey haze. When thoughts of Athena Allard slipped into his mind he took another drink from the bottle.

Suddenly the door burst open and there stood Bone looking twice as big as life in the feminine room of lace and velvet. "I left word at your hotel," the policema[n] snarled, "that I wanted to see you the first thing you g[ot] back to town."

"I got the word, but I had other things to do. Pull up [a] chair, Bone. Sit down. You're workin' yourself into [a] sweat."

The sergeant's big face glowed red. He stepped in[to] the room and slammed the door. He looked about at t[he] gaudy room filled with lace and frills and glass gev[v]-gaws. "So this is what a whore's room looks like," [he] said with a sneer. "You look right at home here, Co[n]cannon."

Concannon sat for a moment, suddenly cold an[d] angry. When he was sure his voice was under control, [he] said, "Bone, these past few days have been tryin' on[es] for me. I'm a little on edge; I'm in no shape to sit he[re] and listen to your insultin' remarks about my friends. [If] you want to talk business, all right. If you don't, get out[.]"

Bone looked as if he had been kicked. His eyes bulge[d.] "Are you drunk, Concannon?"

"Not yet. Not quite."

The detective grunted and moved on into the roor[m.] The feminine character of the room obviously irritate[d] him. "All right," he said at last, sitting on the edge of or[e] of Lily's French chairs, "tell me about Deep Fork. D[id] you talk to Myer?"

"Yes."

"Well?" The sergeant ground his teeth impatientl[y.] "What did he say? Did he tell you where to find A[be] Miller?"

"He didn't know any more about Miller than I did. Except that he's married and has a baby. Did you know that?"

Bone was silent for a moment. "No. What else happened?"

"I killed two men."

The sudden silence was so charged that Satan sat up on the settee and looked first at Concannon and then at Bone. "I think," Bone said with uncharacteristic gentleness, "you'd better start at the first and tell me all about it."

"Their names were Turk and Croy. Does that mean anything to you?"

Bone shook his head.

"The deputy marshal workin' on the case may turn up somethin' later; if he does you'll hear about it in the usual way." Concannon picked up the adventure at the two knolls where the riflemen had tried to bushwhack him and carried it through to the fight on the creek bank.

The sergeant gazed at some invisible spot over Concannon's head, his thoughts far away. At last he said, "You figger this pair of drygulchers knowed somethin' about the robbery?"

"I figure they were part of the gang that took the grass money." Again he told about the meeting of Turk and Croy and Athena Allard and again it chilled him.

Bone's face went hard at the mention of the two thousand dollars that Athena had taken from the outlaws. "Why didn't you tell me about this before?"

"I wanted them to think—for a little while, at least—

that they were safe. That Mrs. Allard had agreed to accept the money and stop pressing the case to clear her husband's name."

"That's withholdin' evidence, Concannon." Bone's voice hissed with anger. "I can have you locked up for that."

Concannon turned the bottle up and drank from the neck. Bone stared at him with bullet eyes and made a visible effort to get himself under control. In due time Concannon picked up the story again and brought it up to the present.

". . . So Mrs. Allard wants you to quit the case," Bone said after a thoughtful silence. "Might be she's right, Concannon. Have you stopped to think about it?"

Concannon looked at him, surprised. "What do you mean?"

Bone smiled his wolfish smile. "You've been on the case how long? A week? Two men are dead, you got your ribs stove in, and almost got yourself bushwhacked. And you still don't know any more about Miller than you did before. Maybe it's time somebody else had a try at it."

"That will be fine with me, just as soon as John Evers gives me my orders."

Bone returned to thoughtful brooding. "I'm still not sure about the two birds you killed. They didn't have any money on them when they died. Why're you so sure they was in on the robbery?"

"They had two thousand dollars to bribe Mrs. Allard with."

There was a sound of breaking furniture from down stairs. One of Lily's dissatisfied customers had started a fight. The brawl spread through the lower floor of the saloon, moving from the gaming tables in back to the bar in front. In the distance there was a sound of police whistles. Concannon and Bone scarcely noticed the disturbance. They sat looking at each other, deeply involved in disturbances of their own.

"I wonder," Concannon said idly, as someone smashed a table downstairs, "just how much does an Oklahoma City police sergeant make in the way of wages, Bone?"

The policeman knew exactly what Concannon was thinking. "Enough to hold body and soul together," he said harshly, "and that's all. If he's honest."

Outside in the street there was a pistol shot. Then a howl, either of pain or rage. Concannon was remembering the way Bone had come to the livery barn to see him off to Deep Fork. He had even selected a saddle animal for him. Someone had alerted Croy and Turk on Concannon's probable line of travel that day—had it been Bone? Had Detective Sergeant Marvin Bone finally become discouraged with trying to live on a policeman's pay and decided to better himself?

Concannon looked directly at the policeman and thought, Are you one of them, Bone? You and Miller and Turk and Croy? If so, where is the money? Where is Miller? In Bunco Alley a squad of police officers had rushed over from their headquarters in City Hall, less than a block away. There was a great commotion as the officers dragged the brawlers off to "Cottonwood de

141

Bastile," as the local wits called their new jailhouse in the alley behind City Hall. Sergeant Bone paid no attention to any of it. He sat back and folded his heavy arms across his chest, the bulge of his .45 digging cruelly into the delicate material of Lily's chair. "You're beginnin' to get a notion, Concannon. I can see it workin'."

Concannon smiled. "I was thinkin' about coincidences, Bone. The way I almost got killed runnin' down a hunch of yours. A hunch that didn't amount to a damn, as it turned out. And the way you selected that gray gelding for me at the livery barn. Why? To make sure there'd be no mistake when the bushwhackers went to work? That's the way it's beginnin' to look to me." He tilted the bottle and looked at it but didn't drink. "Just between the two of us, Bone, with nobody else to hear—is that the way it was? Did you send Turk and Croy to kill me?"

Bone didn't even blink. "Why would I do a thing like that?"

"You must have thought I was dangerous. I don't know why; nothin' I've done has turned out right."

Bone sat breathing in and out through his mouth. He was thinking hard. "That's a dangerous notion to start spreadin' around, Concannon."

"I'm not spreadin' it around. We're just talkin' amongst ourselves, like I said." He tilted the bottle again and this time took a drink. "Did you ever think that police sergeants aren't the only ones that get tired of the job they're saddled with? Do you think a railroad agent's got such a good thing of it?"

Surprisingly, Bone sat back and chuckled. "You're a caution, Concannon. Are you propositionin' me for a share of that grass money?"

"Why not? With Turk and Croy out of the way, there's plenty to go around. Anyway, it's the easiest and simplest way of gettin' rid of me. And you must want to get rid of me, the trouble you went through with Turk and Croy."

Bone's only reaction so far was of dim amusement. "I see. We give you a cut of the cash and you simply pick up and leave. How much do you figger that would be worth?"

Concannon shrugged. "Whatever's fair. Ten thousand dollars?"

"How'd we know you'd hold up your end of the bargain?"

"I could give you a signed receipt for the ten thousand. That would hold me in line."

Bone sat for a while, his face blank. Then he lunged forward in the chair and held out his hand. Surprised, Concannon handed him the bottle. "That's fine tastin' whiskey," the sergeant said with a sigh, turning the bottle up and drinking deeply. "If I was downstairs I never could afford to drink whiskey like this. Everybody'd point and say, 'Look at Marvin Bone, the whores and gamblers have got him on their books.' But I swore I'd never sell out to the whores and gamblers. And I never did." He looked at Concannon and tilted his head and smiled. "But every man has his price. Like you say, we're just talkin' amongst ourselves. Nobody's listenin'.

It don't mean anything." He took another drink and smacked his lips appreciatively. "I had my price. And you've got yours, Concannon . . . but I don't think it's money."

Concannon found that the surface of his skin was tingling. Was this a trick? Or was Bone so confident of himself that he could afford to tell the truth?

"No," the sergeant said thoughtfully, spreading his hands, "I don't think your price is money. I think it's a woman. The widow of your old pal Ray Allard, to get down to facts. Too bad," he sighed. "If it had been money, I could have bought you."

"As it is, you'll have to kill me."

"Maybe I'll have to kill Athena Allard." The sergeant smiled, showing his teeth with all his old savagery. "Unless, of course, you decide to walk off the job."

Concannon felt a cold breath on his neck. There was an eerie air of unreality to this conversation. Concannon could almost believe that in a minute he would wake up and find that it was all a dream. A nightmare. But there was nothing unreal about Marvin Bone. He was the same solid, pugnacious, smart, determined lawman that he had been for years—the perfect model of what a good police sergeant ought to be. Except that he was no longer honest. And he had taken to murder as a sideline.

Suddenly Bone heaved himself out of the chair and dropped the whiskey bottle in Concannon's hand. He shook his heavy head. "Well," he said, as if to himself, "I still think I was right. I kept tellin' him there ain't no use tryin' to scare you off, that sooner or later we'll have to kill you."

Concannon was quick to jump on the word. "You told *who?*"

Bone didn't hear him. Or wouldn't hear him. "Watch out for yourself, Concannon. I'll be goin' now." He hitched at the heavy bulge in his hip pocket and went out of the room.

Concannon heard him going down the stairs, heavy, plodding, tenacious. The man who was going to kill him.

And there was nothing Concannon could do about it. He couldn't go to the police for protection—they would laugh him out of their City Hall headquarters. Marvin Bone, the paragon of honesty and toughness and bravery—who would believe that he was taking bribes, indulging in train robberies and arranging murders?

Concannon was still sitting there with the bottle in his hand when the door opened and Lily came in. "What did you say to Bone? He was lookin' kind of queer when he came down the stairs."

"Sergeant Bone has got things on his mind nowadays."

She squinted at him. "Now that I think on it, you look kind of queer yourself."

"I need some air. Even the air of Bunco Alley," he said, handing her the bottle. "Keep this handy. I'll be back in a little while."

The three-piece Salvation Army band was playing "Throw Out the Lifeline" at the corner of Broadway and Grand. Concannon dropped a quarter into the tambourine, then thought better of it and added a half dollar.

"Lord bless you," the lady bass drummer told him. "You're a fine God-fearin' Christian."

Concannon smiled. It wasn't that he was such a fine God-fearing Christian—but before long he may be in need of a lifeline.

He looked for Bone in the small congregation that surrounded the band. He wasn't there. He wasn't on Bunco Alley or Battle Row or Hop Boulevard. But he was somewhere. And in that heavy .45 revolver in his hip pocket there would be a bullet with the name of Marcus Concannon on it.

He walked along Battle Row and saw a man lying beside a honkytonk, his face covered with blood. It was a thoroughly common sight for that neighborhood, nothing to give a second thought about. Still, there was something . . . That bloody face. It might have been no face at all.

The door of Concannon's mind opened a little. A crack of light appeared; the restless, misshapen thought squirmed into the open. "A closed casket service," the undertaker had complained, when Concannon had asked him about the burial of Ray Allard. Why hadn't Ray's friends been allowed to file past an open casket in the normal way?

For an instant the face of the dead, shotgun-mutilated Croy flashed in his mind, and his insides shrunk. He knew the answer. Or at least he knew where to look for it.

He stepped to the curb and stopped a hack that was turning onto Broadway. "There's a funeral parlor," he told the driver. "On Harvey somewhere. The under-taker's name is . . ."

Suddenly Bone was standing at his elbow. He was grinning his vicious, toothy grin, but his face was strangely pale. "Undertaker, Concannon? Why would you want to see an undertaker this time of night?"

Concannon couldn't think of anything to say. Bone, with a negligent wave of his hand, sent the hack on its way. The loud and reeling citizenry of Battle Row jos-tled them on every side, but Concannon felt as if they were standing alone in a roaring vacuum. Bone stared at him for several seconds, his face hard and expression-less. "You got it figgered out, haven't you?" he said at last.

There was no backing away from it now. No need to talk to the undertaker. Concannon nodded. "I think so."

The policeman shrugged his heavy shoulders and seemed to sigh to himself. "I saw it back at the Day and Night. You was gettin' close." He moved his shoulders again. "Well . . . We might as well get started."

"Started where?"

"You want to talk to him, don't you?"

Concannon showed his surprise. "He's here in Okla-homa City?"

"Not six blocks from where we're standin'." Expertly, the policeman leaned his shoulder against Concannon and quietly hazed him through the crowd. They turned west on Main and walked along the dark, almost deserted street. No one gave them a second glance; they might have been two businessmen returning from a lodge meeting.

"A bird like you," Bone said casually, "ought to of been a gambler. Anybody with your luck."

At that moment Concannon was feeling anything but lucky. His head felt numb. His brain felt like an eight-day clock that somebody had forgotten to wind. "How," he heard himself asking, "do you figure that?"

"You been runnin' in luck ever since you landed in this town." Bone looked at him and shook his head in wonder. "If it had been up to me, I'd of killed you at the beginnin'. Luck. And the way you squirmed out of the trap that Turk and Croy set for you. Pure luck."

"Looks like it's beginnin' to run out now."

Bone chuckled contentedly. He was his old hard, efficient self again. "That's the way it looks, all right."

When they reached the dark corner at Harvey, Bone's big .45 appeared in his hand as if by magic. "I really don't know why you bother to carry this," he chuckled again, skillfully reaching into Concannon's coat and taking the light .38 out of its shoulder holster.

For a while they walked quietly down the middle of the dark, deserted street. Somehow Concannon couldn't bring himself to think about what lay ahead. The questions that had burned his brain a short time ago no longer seemed important. "You're a disappointment to me, Bone," he said at last, only to break the oppressive silence.

Bone looked at him and grinned. "I was an honest policeman for four years. Others was collectin' their pocket money from the pimps and whores and gamblers, but not Marvin Bone. Never a dime. Honest as the day's long." He laughed. "They hate my guts at headquarters."

"What made you stop bein' honest?"

"When there was enough money in it to make it pay." He sighed with self-satisfaction. "I just held my ground and waited. I knew that one day my time would come . . . and it did. One hundred thousand dollars!" He rolled the words lovingly in his mouth. "Makes your head swim, don't it?"

"How many do you have to divide it with?"

"Just the two of us, me and him. Lookin' back on it, you did us a big favor by killin' Turk and Croy. Saved one of us from havin' to do it."

Concannon could almost feel sorry for Turk and Croy. All the trouble they had gone to, and it had never been in the cards for them to take a split of that grass money.

They had reached the shabby end of Harvey, next to the rambling Frisco freight house. Bone nudged Concannon along a dirt path toward a shack sitting well back from the street in a patch of dead weeds. "Not much of a home, is it?" the sergeant asked conversationally. "But it's the best a policeman can do, if he's honest." He hesitated, then stepped quickly to the door and knocked. "It's me, Bone. I've got Concannon with me"

There was a moment of electric silence. Concannon could almost hear the racing of a brain on the other side of the door. Then a voice, surprisingly faint and toneless, said, "All right, come on in."

Bone fumbled with a key and unlocked the door. They stepped inside and Bone quickly slammed the door and bolted it. For a moment it was as dark as a dungeon Someone was breathing lightly, shallowly, wheezing slightly. The sound made Concannon's scalp prickle.

There was an explosion of light as Bone struck a sulphur match and lit a bracket lamp beside the door. A man, propped up on a folded saddle blanket, lay on a homemade bunk against the far wall. He held a single-action .45 in both hands, the muzzle wavering slightly as he aimed it at Concannon's chest. He said to Bone, "Did you get the pistol out of his shoulder holster?"

Bone grinned and showed him the .38.

With a nod of satisfaction, the man lowered his own weapon. With a small, faraway smile, he said, "Well Marcus, you haven't changed much."

Concannon heard himself saying, "You have, Ray."

CHAPTER 9

Ray Allard had once been a man of commanding strength and vigor. There had been an irrepressible good humor in his eyes and spring steel in his limbs. Now he lay limp, his face sagging and pale as tallow. His skin dry as ashes, clung to the bones of his face like shrinking rawhide. His eyes were bright with fever.

Bone folded his heavy arms across his chest and leaned against the door facing, watching with interest this reunion of two old friends. "He was about to figger it out," the policeman told Allard. "Catchin' a hack to the undertaker's when I stopped him."

Allard nodded and managed a heatless smile. "I fig-

150

ured it would come to you," he told Concannon, "sooner or later. Who was it started you thinkin'? The undertaker?"

Concannon nodded. "Somethin' he said about a closed casket funeral service. Only one reason for a service like that—when the man in the box is in no shape to be looked at." He fumbled for a cigar, bit off the end and lit it. "Who was it in that box, Ray? The nitroglycerin expert, Miller?"

Allard nodded, his feverish eyes on Concannon's face. "Ab Miller. He was my build. Even had the same color hair. Well, a shotgun, as you know, is not the neatest weapon in the world, but at close range it does the job better than any. Miller took a load of buckshot at point-blank range—that's why they didn't open the casket at the funeral." He smiled faintly, almost dreamily. "It wasn't a bad funeral, everything considered. Hothouse flowers on the grave. Important people. John Evers was there. Even the mayor was there. Tell you the truth, Marcus, I was a little disappointed that you wasn't there."

"I was busy," Concannon said dryly. "There was never any suspicion that the wrong man was gettin' buried?"

"Why should there be any suspicion? Miller was wearin' my clothes and had my things in his pockets. Who would suspect that he wasn't Ray Allard?"

"Your wife, maybe."

For a moment Allard's face was as expressionless as stone. Then he shrugged wearily. "No, not Athena. Since there was no doubt in anybody's mind that I was the dead man, she wasn't asked to identify the body." Again that expressionless mask settled on his face. "Well," he said after a moment, "that's not quite right. There was one that saw through the little game and knew that Ray Allard was not the body in the casket."

"I think I can guess," Concannon said flatly. "Detective Sergeant Marvin Bone."

Still lounging against the doorframe, Bone chuckled. Concannon ignored the policeman and said, "Bone wasn't in on the actual robbery?"

"Didn't know anything about it till it was all over. But he's a policeman, our Sergeant Bone. Got a policeman's nose, and he smelled somethin' wrong. He went to the crewmen on the train and started askin' questions. Then to Athena, and finally the undertaker. I knew then it was only a matter of time before he caught up to me"

"So you went to him first, with a proposition to divide the grass money."

Allard started to grin but a sudden pain caused his face to go white. "That goddam mail clerk on the train!" he gasped after a moment. "Jerked a pistol out of a mail sack and shot me in the belly even before Miller had a chance to open the safe. Well," he grated, "there's nothin' to be done about that now. Turk shot him on the spot."

"Then you shotgunned Miller, after he opened the safe, and dressed the body in your clothes?"

Allard made a wheezing sound. "It was Miller's hard luck that he happened to look like me. You've got to admit it was a good scheme. We got away slick with a hundred thousand dollars, and nobody's even lookin' for me, because they think I'm dead."

"Except for me."

Allard gestured weakly. "You don't count, Marcus. We're friends. We've been through too much together." He didn't actually mention the time that he had saved Concannon's life, but he made sure that it hadn't slipped Concannon's mind. Those feverish eyes were studying him gravely. "You wouldn't turn me in, would you, Marcus?"

"You're a murderer now."

"Miller? That was a matter of survival. He would have done the same to me."

"You planned it and killed him in cold blood and then passed the body off as your own."

Allard licked his dry lips. "Well, have it your own way. But you owe me somethin', Marcus. I didn't want to mention it, but now I've got to. If it wasn't for me you wouldn't be here now. You'd be a long time dead."

"I thought we'd get to that," Concannon said coldly.

"All this talk," Bone said impatiently, "is startin' to make my head ache. I know his kind—he won't listen to reason. Let me kill him now and be done with it."

A chilly smile touched the corners of Ray Allard's mouth. "There you are, Marcus. Bone knows what he's talkin' about. You're a danger to us, and he's convinced that killin' you is the only way out."

"What do you think, Ray?"

Allard gazed up at the ceiling of the shack. "Bone, leave us alone for a while. We want to talk. It's personal."

153

The sergeant scowled. "I don't like it, the shape you're in."

"Leave us alone," Allard repeated wearily.

Bone hitched at his heavy .45. "All right. But I still don't like it."

When the policeman was out of the shack, Concannon said dryly, "You've got Bone trained like a spotted dog in a circus. A few days ago I would have said that was impossible."

Allard smiled. "Money," he said. "Anything is possible with money . . . Do you want money, Marcus?"

"Not that grass money. It's too messed up with blood."

"Don't be a trial to me, Marcus," Allard said with a ghostly smile. "I've got fire in my guts and my brain's buzzin' like a nest of yellowjackets. I want your word that you'll walk off the case. You owe me that much. But that will settle your debt." He raised a hand and pointed to the corner of the shack. "Over there somewhere, behind the saddlebags, there's a bottle of whiskey. Get it; we'll have a drink for old-times' sake."

Concannon got the bottle and they drank from the neck, gravely, solemnly. "Marcus, what do you say?"

"Do I have a choice?"

"Well," Allard admitted, "there's Bone to be considered. A dangerous man when he's aggravated."

Concannon held out his hands in a gesture of helplessness. "Like you say, I guess I owe you that much."

There was an obvious show of relief in Allard's pale face. "I knew I could depend on you. Turk and Croy, and then Bone, they all wanted to kill you. That's the only

154

thing they could think of. But I told them, 'When the time comes, Marcus and me will come to an understandin'.' I was right, wasn't I?"

"It looks that way." Concannon pulled up a cane-bottom chair and sat down beside the bed. "Have you seen a doctor about that bullet in your guts?"

"Sure, Turk found one for me. Not exactly a doctor, an old Shawnee woman that doctors with herbs and bark and things like that. I'm gettin' better. In another week I'll be away from here."

"Why did you send Bone away? What's so personal that he couldn't listen."

Allard smiled sheepishly, and for just a moment he looked impish and boyish and nothing more. "Tell you the truth, I guess I'm just tired of lookin' at Bone's ugly face. Turk and Croy and Miller, when they was alive, wasn't much better. That's one thing I've learned—the worst thing about bein' an outlaw is the company a man has to keep."

He went through the motions of laughing at his little joke, but no sound came from his mouth.

"Why did you take to outlawin', Ray?"

"The money," he said with a sigh. "I got sick of scratchin' in the gravel like a chicken—I wanted somethin' more than that." For a moment he looked puzzled. He shook his head. "Funny thing is, I can't remember exactly what it was. Just the money, I guess. It seemed like the most important thing in the world. And there it was, in the same coach I'd be ridin' in, and it was such an easy thing to get a bunch together. Two toughs, Turk and Croy. And Ab Miller to blow the safe open. I didn't have to ask them twice, any of them. They wanted that money as much as I did."

"Where's the money now?"

Allard hesitated. "In a safe place," he said slowly. "Nobody but me knows where. That's how I've managed to stay alive this long."

"That's not easy to believe. Why would Turk and Croy allow you to get away with all the money?"

"It was all part of the plan," Allard groaned. "Do the job as fast as possible, then split up and meet later at a place on the Washita that I'd picked out." He lay for a moment thinking about the robbery, the angry crewmen, the train bristling with guns. "Things was gettin' hot," he went on. "I grabbed the money and lit out. That's all there was to it. At the time I never figured I was hurt so bad—just a hot ache in the guts, that's all. I soon learned better. If I aimed to stay alive I had to hide that money— I had to give Turk and Croy a good reason for keepin' me in good health. Until they got their hands on that money, anyhow."

"Where did you hide it?"

Allard smiled bleakly and shook his head. "That's one thing I can't tell you, Marcus. It's my insurance. As long as I'm the only one to know, I can be sure that Sergeant Bone will look after me."

"You didn't hide all of it. Turk and Croy gave two thousand dollars to your wife and five hundred to Maggie Slatter."

Allard's face was gray and expressionless. "I'll tell

you somethin', Marcus—I never was cut out to be an outlaw. I don't know why; maybe because I worked too long on the other side. But you've got to believe that I never aimed to kill anybody. That's the reason I kept out part of that money." He shook his head again and looked truly puzzled. "Five hundred dollars! To a whore like Maggie Slatter, that was a fortune. You'd think she'd take it and be thankful, and that would be the end of it, wouldn't you. But no, she began talkin' to you about Miller. Pretty soon she'd have started talkin' to the police, and everything would have gone to hell."

"So you had Turk and Croy kill her."

"Nothin' for it. She didn't leave me a choice."

"What about your wife, Ray? Do you intend to kill her too?"

Those feverish eyes stared at Concannon. "You know better than that. I was hopin' she would take the money and somehow guess that I would come for her one day, and everything would be all right again."

There was a hollow ring in Concannon's voice. "You still love her then. I was beginnin' to think you didn't."

Allard looked as if the suggestion startled him. "I love Athena more than anything in the world; nothin' will ever change that."

"The last time I saw her she was putting flowers on your grave. Her eyes were red; she had been crying."

"I don't want to talk about that now. Not about Athena." Allard closed his eyes for a moment. When he opened them again they were glassy with exhaustion. "I've been honest with you, Marcus. I've told

157

you everything there is to know."

"Not quite. There's the little matter of the murdered pimp. I know it's almost too small a thing to even mention," he said bitterly, "but you know how it is with old lawmen. Curious."

"Nothin' to it." The thin shoulders shrugged. "He listened outside Maggie's crib when you talked to her. Well, pimps know everything—or think they do. He circulated the word that a railroad agent was askin' questions about Miller, so I sent Turk and Croy to talk to him." He shook his head sadly. "The pimp was greedy; he wanted a share of that grass money."

"So you killed him"

"If I started dividin' up the money amongst everybody that wanted it, there'd be nothin' left for me."

Concannon smiled, but his face felt as if it were cracking. "So you're the one that was never cut out to be an outlaw. You're a caution, Ray."

"It's the truth," Allard objected. "I wanted to do the right thing by that pimp, but he wouldn't listen. Neither would Maggie."

"Neither would I. I wonder why you didn't have me killed, Ray, instead of merely ordering your two toughs to kick my ribs in."

Allard looked truly appalled at such a suggestion. "You're my friend, Marcus. Do you think I'd kill a friend?"

"You killed Ab Miller."

"He wasn't my friend. Anyway, that was a special situation. It couldn't be helped." He lay still for a while, breathing shallowly, looking like a frail old man. "All the same," he admitted at last, "it was a mistake lettin' Turk and Croy beat you that way. I should have known that you wouldn't be scared off. I would have known, if I had been myself. But my guts were on fire and I was mad. I'm sorry, Marcus."

"Well, I'm still alive," Concannon said dryly. "I guess I ought to be thankful for that."

Allard smiled, and for just an instant he looked like his old self. "Like I said, Marcus, I never was cut out to be an outlaw. When all this is over it will be different."

"What will it be like for your wife?"

Allard set his jaw with a kind of thoughtless stubbornness. "Athena will be all right; she comes from tough stock. She'll wait for me."

"She thinks you're dead."

"With her head, maybe. In her heart she knows better. She knows I'll come for her when I can. As soon as I can."

"But in the meantime you'll let her grieve over the body in your grave."

Allard sighed. There was a whole lifetime of weariness in the sound. "I don't want to talk about that now. All I want is your word that you'll quit the case and forget you ever knew me."

"That's all you want," Concannon mimicked bitterly. "It will mean losing my job—the only decent job I ever had. You know that."

"I know. Do I have your word?"

Concannon could see five years of hard work going up

in the kind of smoke that wishes and dreams are mad
of. The hard work, the years of friendship, the face of
woman that he couldn't get out of his brain—all of
being snatched away on a relentless wind. "You've g
my word."

"Knock three times on the door," Allard said.

Concannon did it. Almost immediately the doc
opened and Detective Sergeant Bone reentered th
shack. "It's all over," Allard told the policeman. "Giv
him back his .38."

Bone looked outraged. "Are you out of your head?"

"Give him his pistol. I've got his word. Marcus is qui
ting the case."

Bone's broad sneer said what he thought of the wor
of a railroad agent. But he grudgingly handed over th
weapon and Concannon returned it to its holster.

"Marcus . . ." Allard said as Concannon was about t
leave. Then his thoughts seemed to drift. He licked h
dry lips and visibly pulled himself together. "How we
do you know my wife, Marcus?"

Concannon was surprised by the question. "Not ver
well. I've talked to her three times."

"She's the only woman I ever loved." That seemed t
be all he wanted to say. He reached for the whiske
bottle, took a drink and gazed dully into space. Cor
cannon left the shack.

It was midmorning, almost thirty-six hours after th
meeting with Ray Allard, when the knock came at th
door of Concannon's hotel room. It was loud, imperiou

angry. It could belong only to one man.

Concannon opened the door and said, "Come in, Mr. Evers. I was just about to leave."

John Evers plunged into the room in a rich cloud of Cuban cigar smoke, like a heavy Baldwin under a full head of steam. Angrily, he shook a yellow telegram under Concannon's nose. "What's the meaning of this idiocy? Do you realize that I was in conference with a very important board member when this message reached me in Chicago? Do you in the slightest way appreciate the awkwardness of the position you've placed me in? Do you realize that I've been ridin' trains for two nights and a day to get here in time, I hope, to save you from this unexplainable insanity?"

Concannon said, "Sit down, Mr. Evers. I thought the telegram explained everything. I'm quitting my job with the railroad—that's all there is to it."

"I don't want to sit down!" the chief inspector roared. He glared at the tip of his cigar. In his anger he had smoked it too fast and the dappled wrapper was beginning to curl. With considerable effort and force of will, he took himself in hand. "All right, Concannon. Start at the beginning. Tell me everything."

"There's not much to tell. I've been beaten and kicked unconscious. Two people have been killed, more or less on my account, and I've killed two men myself. I guess I'm just gettin' too old for the work."

"Nonsense!" Evers snarled. "Being a lawman is all you know, it's all you'll ever be. What did you find out at Deep Fork?"

161

Concannon told him about the misadventure in detail. Evers looked thoughtful. He breathed lightly on the tip of his cigar, but it would not burn to suit him so he put it on the edge of the black oak dresser and forgot it. "This Miller," he said slowly. "Sometimes I wonder if there ever was such a man."

"There was. He left his women behind to prove it."

"Then where is he? He's the key to this unpleasant business, but he might as well be dead and buried for all the good he's doing us."

Dead and buried. Concannon smiled bleakly.

"Find him," Evers said shortly. "Find him and get to the bottom of this thing; the board members are rapidly running out of patience."

Concannon shook his head with real regret. Evers's face and tone turned suddenly hard. "You walk off this job and I'll see that you never get another one—with the railroad or anywhere else."

"I'm sorry, but that's a chance I'll have to take."

The inspector reached back into his long experience and fired a shot in the dark. "Is it the woman? Allard's widow? Did she somehow talk you off the case?" With lively interest he watched the color go out of Concannon's face. Has it occurred to you that she and Allard could have been in this thing together? That she wants you off the case so that she can then safely pick up the money, wherever it is, and go on her way a rich and merry widow?"

"I'm catchin' the northbound to Kansas City at two o'clock," Concannon told him dully. "I'm sorry the job

162

didn't work out. I liked workin' for the railroad."

"You'll never work for it again," Evers promised.

Bone was waiting on the sidewalk when Concannon came out of the hotel with his grips. "I saw John Evers go up to your room. What did he want?"

"The same thing you want," Concannon told him. "The money." A hack driver, seeing Concannon standing in front of the hotel with the suitcases at his feet, reined smartly up to the sidewalk. "Take these to the Santa Fe depot," Concannon told him. "I'll pick them up later." He started walking north toward Main.

Bone fell in beside him. "What train you catchin'?"

"The two o'clock to Kansas City."

The detective grinned. "Tell you the truth, I figgered all along I'd have to kill you before everything was settled. Even after that get-together with your old pal. Now it looks like you're really fixin' to pull out. I can't say I'm sorry." He bared his teeth in the wolfish manner that suited him perfectly. "I kind of like you, Concannon, all things considered. I wouldn't of taken any pleasure in shootin' you down."

"That's fine," Concannon told him sourly. "I wouldn't want to put you out any."

Bone chuckled as he ambled along, occasionally hitching at the .45 in his hip pocket. "Tell me somethin', to settle my curiosity. What did Allard say that got you to drop the case?"

Concannon looked straight ahead and said nothing. Bone shrugged. "Well, it ain't important. Just curiosity."

They crossed the street at Main and headed east toward Robinson. The sergeant took Concannon's arm in a grip of iron. Suddenly he was no longer the chuckling, amiable policeman that he had been a moment before—he was a desperate man on the grim trail of one hundred thousand dollars. "One thing more, Concannon." They stopped dead still in the middle of the sidewalk. "If you're headed for the Fine and Dandy Cafe, forget it."

Concannon looked at him in surprise. "Why?"

"Because I promised Allard I'd watch out for that wife of his and see that you don't bother her." Once again he grinned coldly and shook his head. "Seems like your old pal don't trust you around his wife. Can't say that I blame him, the moon-eyed way you look at her."

"Is that what you've come to, Bone?" Concannon asked dryly. "A police officer runnin' errands for an outlaw? When Ray Allard snaps his fingers, Marvin Bone jumps—is that what you've come to?"

But Bone would not be led down that dangerous path. He merely smiled. "I don't mind a little jumpin', all things considered. Why don't you go to the depot and wait for the train? Save everybody a heap of trouble."

Concannon shook his head. "Between now and train time I'll go where I want to go and do whatever suits me."

Bone scowled and set his jaw belligerently. "Don't you get fancy with me, Concannon."

"You go tell Ray that a smart gambler doesn't try to stretch his luck. Tell him I'm keepin' my part of the bargain—be satisfied with that."

CHAPTER 10

It was the dinner hour and should have been the busiest time of the day, but the cafe was less than half filled. Word was getting around, Concannon thought to himself, about Pat Duncan's cooking.

He took a table in front of the plate-glass window and watched Athena Allard as she moved quickly, gracefully from customer to customer. When she came to Concannon she looked at him blankly at first, then smiled faintly. "The fried steak is good. Or the chicken, if there's any left."

"I'm leavin' Oklahoma City in a little while." He shrugged and made himself smile. "I just came by to say goodbye, but I might as well eat while I'm at it. The steak."

"You're leaving." She sounded relieved to hear it. She stood for a moment with a faraway look in her eyes. "Yes," she said at last, "that's best. I'll get your steak now."

He ate slowly, watching the Robinson Street activity from his window table. Across the street, in the doorway of a hardware store, a familiar dark-clad figure stood like a cigar-store Indian watching the cafe. John Evers. Concannon was faintly surprised that the inspector had followed him from the hotel and was now keeping watch on him. Why? He no longer worked for the railroad. He had quit, and that should have been the end of it. But he should have known that things were never that simple with a man like Evers.

Well, he thought grimly, to hell with John Evers. He ate his steak, tough and stringy as it was, to the last bite. By that time the dinner hour was over and the cafe was almost empty. Athena came to his table with a pot of coffee. "There's apple pie. Or chocolate cake, but the cake's yesterday's."

Concannon declined dessert but accepted another cup of coffee. "Mrs. Allard . . ." It seemed ridiculous to go on calling her Mrs. Allard, but somehow he couldn't bring himself to call her anything else. "Mrs. Allard, can I talk to you a minute?"

She glanced at Pat Duncan and the cook shrugged and feigned indifference. "All right, Mr. Concannon."

"The thing is," Concannon began awkwardly, "I'm not workin' for the railroad any more. I'm goin' back to Kansas City to see if I can find somethin' else up there. Well, I remember you sayin' that you aimed to go back to your folks in Kansas. And I was thinkin' . . ." It occurred to him that this was probably the most ridiculous speech that he had ever made. Athena Allard was watching him gravely without having the faintest notion of what he was getting at. "I was thinkin' that—after things get settled some—it might be that someday I'd get a chance to see you. If I happened to be in that part of the country, that is. And if you didn't mind, of course." To hell with Ray Allard. He had settled his debt to Ray, and Athena had no part in it.

For a moment he thought that she wasn't going to say anything at all. She merely looked at him with that

166

blankness that he had come to expect of her. Then a hint of a smile touched her lips and she seemed to sigh. "I've been a great deal of trouble to you, haven't I, Mr. Concannon? I realize that now, and I'm sorry. But at the time it seemed . . ." She groped for the right words. "It seemed that I just couldn't make myself believe that Ray was dead. Still, his good name was all I had left of him, and I wanted to save it. I wanted that more than anything else in the world. It sounds silly, doesn't it?"

"No ma'am, it doesn't sound that at all."

"Silly," she said again, gazing absently across the street. "I've come to realize it now. Ray's dead. There's nothing—nothing at all—that can be done about it." She returned her gaze to Concannon. "I'll be leaving Oklahoma City too, before long. Maybe tomorrow, if Pat can find another girl for the cafe."

"To Kansas?"

"To Kansas," she echoed.

Concannon cleared his throat and tried again. "About what I was sayin', ma'am. After some time passes, after you get yourself settled, would you mind if an ex-railroad man came callin'?"

She smiled sadly. "It wouldn't do any good, Mr. Concannon. It would just be a waste of time."

"Time's one thing I've got plenty of right now." He lurched up from the table, not giving her another chance to turn him down. "I hope you have a good trip, ma'am. And that things will be all right for you." He left the cafe feeling a fool.

He crossed the street, dodging town rigs and dray

167

wagons, and made for that still, dark figure in the hardware store doorway. "I wonder how you ever got to be an inspector," Concannon told Evers flatly, "when you can't even track a man on a city street without bein' spotted."

Evers smiled and puffed comfortably on his cigar. "I've been doing some thinking about you, Concannon," he said, ignoring the professional slur. "I should have noticed it before, but there were other things on my mind." He paused and inspected his cigar to make sure it was burning to suit him. "What kind of scheme have you got cooking with Marvin Bone?"

Concannon blinked. "What do you mean?"

"I mean, when a railroad agent spends as much time as you do with a crooked police officer, it's something for a railroad inspector to think about."

For a moment Concannon could think of nothing to say. Until recently he had been absolutely convinced of Bone's honesty, so he had assumed that others had thought the same way. It was always a mistake to underestimate a man like John Evers. "What," he asked, "makes you think Bone's crooked?"

Evers shrugged. "I get a feeling about people. In a town of crooked policemen, Bone is too honest for his own good. I get the feeling he's waiting for something. And then . . ." He snapped his fingers. "Like a steel trap in your path, you're caught. Did you get yourself caught in that trap, Concannon?"

Concannon watched him closely. "You're not drunk, are you, Mr. Evers?"

"I never get drunk, Concannon. And I don't like to let go of a good man, if I can help it. It's not too late to straighten yourself out with the railroad."

Concannon smiled. "At what price?"

"Tell me what's going on between you and Bone. Does it have to do with the robbery?"

This, Concannon thought, was dangerous ground. Best to back away from it fast. "Goodbye, Mr. Evers. At two o'clock I'll be on the northbound for Kansas City. If you think I had anything to do with the robbery you can wire the police officials there." He wheeled and started to walk toward Broadway.

The inspector fell in beside him, matching his long stride with ease. "You're a fool, Concannon," he said mildly. "The mail clerk was killed in that robbery, remember. Don't make yourself an accessory to murder."

"Is that what you think? That I killed that mail clerk? I was on a job in St. Louis at the time."

"You know what I mean. Money, big money, does queer things to people. Maybe you and Bone think you can grab that money for yourselves. But it's a mistake, Concannon, thinking you can get away with it."

Concannon stepped quickly to the curb and waved down a passing hack. "I'm goin' to the depot to wait for my train. I'd rather wait by myself, if you don't mind."

John Evers shook his head sadly. "When it's all over just remember that I gave you a second chance and you turned it down. You won't get another."

Concannon directed the driver to take the long way

169

around to the Santa Fe depot. He didn't want to see the Half Acre again. There were too many gritty, against-the-grain memories there. Too many reminders of opportunities lost. He paid the driver at the depot, picked up his grips and took a seat on a baggage cart to wait. The clock inside the ticket agent's cubicle said ten past one. Fifty minutes would see the end of it.

He sat there for what seemed a long time, surrounded by gossiping, tobacco-chewing, stick-whittling loafers who seemed never to miss a train arrival or departure. He listened to the fitful clattering of the telegraph receiver. He breathed in the heady smell of cinders and soot and green crossties oozing pitch. It was a mild day for October. It would have been a fine day, except that he was out of a job, the prospects of finding another were poor, his friend was a murderer, and the one woman who haunted his thoughts wouldn't give him a second glance. He smiled grimly and lit a cigar. Yes sir, a fine day, except for those few imperfections.

He got up and checked the bulletin board to see if the train was on time. It was. The clock in the agent's office said one thirty-five. Twenty-five minutes to go. He returned to the baggage cart and finished his cigar.

A voice at his elbow said, "Mr. Concannon . . . please help me."

Startled, he turned and stared at Athena Allard. Her face was as pale as death, her eyes wide. She was holding out an envelope. "Please," she said again, "help me."

Concannon took the envelope almost without realizing

that he did so. "A boy brought this to the cafe just a few minutes ago," she said in a taut voice that was little more than a whisper. "I . . . didn't know what to do or where to turn. You're the only one I could think of."

He opened the envelope and looked at it quickly. There was money. How much money he couldn't tell without counting it, but the bills were new and crisp and clean. He had seen that kind of money before. "What boy gave you this?"

"Just a boy. I don't know. He said a man gave it to him and told him to bring it to me at the cafe."

There was something in the envelope besides the money. A train ticket to a small water stop in the Chickasaw Nation. And a note. Three lines on a piece of brown wrapping paper.

Take this train ticket and go to where it says. Wait there for me. It won't be long. Don't say anything to anybody.

It wasn't signed, but Concannon recognized the handwriting. "Do you know who this is from?"

"Of course, it's from Ray!" she said in that curiously taut, fiddlestring-twangy voice. "He's alive!"

Concannon took a deep breath and tried to think. But his head was a roaring vacuum. He couldn't imagine Ray doing a thing so foolish, jeopardizing himself just when he had the hundred thousand dollars almost in his hands. He heard himself saying dumbly, "Ma'am, I think we better think about this a minute. We don't actually know that this is from Ray at all."

"It's Ray's handwriting! I know it!" She was on the verge of hysteria. She covered her face with her hands and made a visible effort to take hold of herself. The depot loafers had stopped their gossiping and whittling and spitting and were watching them curiously. Suddenly Concannon didn't like so much attention.

"Come in the depot," he said, taking her arm. She allowed him to lead her into the depot, but she wouldn't sit down. She stood rigidly, her clenched fists at her side, looking like a woman who was about to start screaming. "All right," Concannon said quietly, soothingly, as if he were speaking to a frightened colt. "Try to take it easy, ma'am. Try to get it straight just what happened. Whatever it is, we'll get to the bottom of it."

Slowly, she began to unwind. But she still wouldn't sit down. "I'm sorry . . ." She shuddered. "But all this time . . ." Suddenly her eyes widened and in them Concannon saw terror. "If Ray's alive, who's buried in his grave?"

"That's somethin' we'll think about when we come to it," Concannon evaded. "Now think a minute. About the boy that brought this envelope. Have you ever seen him before?"

"I'm . . . not sure. He was just a boy, about twelve years old, with sandy hair." She began to grow taut again. "How could it have happened? How could Ray be alive all this time and never let me know?"

That, Concannon thought to himself, is somethin' I'd give a good deal to know myself. Aloud he said, "Other than those two men that you told me about, has anybody threatened you or tried to frighten you?"

She started to shake her head, then frowned. "There was a man. But he didn't threaten me."

"Who was that?" The question came sharply.

"A policeman," she said, "by the name of Bone."

Concannon took a deep breath. Bone. Yes, it must be making Bone nervous having Allard's "widow" underfoot, and never quite knowing how much she knew or suspected about her husband's part in the robbery.

A half-formed thought crossed Concannon's mind and left him chilled. In the past few days he had learned a great deal about Marvin Bone. He was a man with a single thought in his head—that hundred thousand dollars. He was prepared to kill for it. Concannon had no doubt that he would kill Athena, if he was convinced that she stood between him and the money.

"What," he asked, "did Bone say to you?"

"Well . . ." She collected her thoughts. "He said there were ugly rumors about Ray's part in the robbery. He said that by just being here I was helping to keep the rumors alive. He didn't actually tell me to leave Oklahoma City, but that was what he meant."

"What else?"

"That's all, except . . ." A shadow crossed behind her eyes. "He watches. Sometimes I see him watching the cafe from across the street. When I leave the cafe I see him when I turn a corner, in a doorway, or maybe just standing on the sidewalk, looking."

"Was he there when the boy brought this envelope?"

"I didn't look. I was thinking only of Ray."

"Does anyone else know about the envelope?"

"Only Pat Duncan, the cook at the cafe."

A dozen possibilities whirled in Concannon's mind, none of them pleasant. In the distance he could hear the two o'clock northbound approaching the switches.

Athena looked at him worriedly. "Is something the matter?"

He avoided the question and asked one of his own. "If Sergeant Bone went to Pat Duncan and asked him about that note, would Duncan tell him what was in it?"

She started to say no, then changed her mind and nodded. "Yes, I guess he would. Sergeant Bone is a . . ."

"A persuasive man," Concannon finished wryly.

And a curious one. If he had seen the boy delivering that envelope, Bone's natural policeman's curiosity would have swelled to the bursting point. He would have gone directly to Pat Duncan and demanded to know what the envelope had contained. And Duncan would have told him—because cooks in cafes like the Fine and Dandy did not withhold information from policemen like Bone.

Athena watched with growing alarm as Concannon pursued his unpleasant thoughts. He tried to imagine the thoughts that would pass through the policeman's mind when he learned about the envelope. Bone's first thought would be that Ray was planning to double-cross him, setting up a meeting with his wife in the Chickasaw Nation, near the site of the robbery. Near the place where Ray must have hidden the money.

What would Bone do then? He couldn't kill Ray, because Ray was the only one who knew where the money was. But he might very well kill Athena, if he was convinced that she and Ray were scheming to do him out of his share of the grass money.

Something of Concannon's anxiety must have shown in his face, for Athena instinctively pulled away from him when he took her arm. He said as calmly as he could, "I don't like the feel of things here. I think we ought to go."

She was beginning to look indignant and angry. "Mr. Concannon I was hoping you'd help me, because of you and Ray . . . But if you don't want to . . ."

"I want to help you. But I think we'd better get away from this depot before the train comes in."

He took her arm firmly and led her toward the door. But at the doorway he froze. Sergeant Marvin Bone was coming down the tracks from the direction of Broadway, walking fast and slightly bent over, as if he were moving against a stiff wind. Concannon tightened his hold on Athena's arm.

"Mr. Concannon, you're hurting me!"

"I'm sorry. But we've got to go now." He pulled her across the depot waiting room and, without a word, kicked open the door to the ticket agent's office.

A small man with glistening bald head was copying something from the telegram receiver. Startled, he turned to stare at Concannon and the woman.

Before he had a chance to object Concannon and Athena Allard had crossed the ticket office and entered the baggage room. Concannon dragged her stumbling through a maze of trunks and boxes. "Mr. Concannon,

175

I demand to know . . ."

"Later, ma'am," he said shortly. "Walk as fast as you can, we'll be out of here in a minute."

From the baggage room they entered a long freight shed. The area behind the shed was crowded with dray wagons and commercial hacks waiting for disembarking train passengers. "This way," Concannon said, pulling Athena along with him through the clutter of teams and rigs. The northbound to Kansas City was wheezing and releasing steam, huffing slowly into the station.

Concannon slanted south now at an easy lope, pulling Athena along with him over the rutted hitching area behind the depot. Athena was gasping, almost sobbing for breath.

Concannon would not allow her to rest. They reached Front Street and ducked behind the row of shacks, out of sight of the depot. At last they came to that eastern arm of California Avenue known as Alabaster Row. Concannon half-dragged, half-carried her to the dirt walk in front of a barbecue house and allowed her to get her breath.

She stared at him angrily. "Mr. Concannon . . . ! Have you lost your mind!"

"No ma'am, I don't think so. I think you're in danger. If I'm right, it was necessary to get away from the depot in a hurry."

She glared at him, bristling. "Why?" she demanded.

"It's a long story." And an ugly one, he thought silently. "Have you got your breath now?"

She nodded but did not look convinced that he was

completely sane. A huge black man with a long knife scar on his left cheek came out of the barbecue house and eyed them with suspicion and hostility. It was not often that white folks came to Alabaster Row—white women, almost never. "Mister," the black man told Concannon softly, "I don't know what your trouble is, but I reckon you better take it someplace away from here."

Concannon dug in his pocket and found ten dollars. He handed it to the black man. "Take me to Miss Annie Bee's place. I'm a friend of hers. There won't be any trouble."

The black man looked doubtful—still, ten dollars was ten dollars. "If you're lyin' to me, mister, Miss Annie's boys'll chew you up like a pack of coon dogs."

"I know," Concannon told him with some feeling.

The man shrugged and pocketed the money. "This way." He slipped into a narrow passageway between the barbecue house and the next building. Concannon and Athena followed. They stumbled through the cluttered alleyways that lay behind California Avenue. At last they stopped. "This here's as far as I go," their guide said, pointing to the rear of a two-story house just ahead. "The rest is between you and Miss Annie Bee."

Athena was clutching Concannon's arm, staring about her with wide eyes, as if she could not make herself believe the things that were happening to her. Concannon smiled fleetingly and took her hand. "It'll be all right. Annie's an old friend." They went up to the door and Concannon knocked.

The door opened and a young girl with amazingly cool

eyes stared at them. "Tell Miss Annie Bee that Concannon's here. He wants to talk to her," Concannon told her.

A second woman pushed the girl aside and opened the door wide. She had been a beautiful girl once, a long while ago. Her face was still as smooth and black as polished jet. She began to smile when she recognized Concannon. "Well now, whereabouts did you spring from, Marshal?"

"I'm not a marshal any more, Annie. But I've got a little trouble. Can we come in?"

"Trouble?" Her smile was not quite so warm.

"Not police trouble, Annie. Personal. We won't bother you long, but right now we need a place to sit and think." He wanted to stop there, but he knew that Annie could get all the details in a matter of minutes, if she wanted them. "I'll tell you the truth, Annie. The trouble's with Marvin Bone. But it's personal, not police trouble."

"Marvin Bone's a policeman." Miss Annie Bee was growing cooler by the second.

"Annie," Concannon told her quietly, "you owe me a favor. Or doesn't your memory go back that far?" It was time for collecting debts. Ray collected from Concannon, Concannon collected from Annie.

Reluctantly, the black woman stepped out of the doorway. "I guess it'll be all right. But just for a little while."

"Thanks, Annie. I won't forget it."

She looked at him as if he were a stranger, and not a very attractive one at that. "The only thanks I want is for you *not* to remember. You can sit here in the kitchen; there won't nobody bother you."

Concannon and Athena stepped into a small white-washed kitchen. It smelled of woodsmoke and coffee and strong tobacco. Annie left them alone for a moment, then came back with a bottle of whiskey and put it on an oilcloth-covered table. "How long do you expect you'll be?"

"We'd like to stay till it's dark, Annie, then we'll go."

Annie made no secret of not liking it, but she said, "All right, just till dark. I don't fool with Marvin Bone any more'n I can help" She left them again and this time closed the kitchen door.

In some distant part of the house they could hear the rattle of dice, the laughter of men, and of women. Athena Allard did not seem to notice any of it. Still out of breath and stunned by Concannon's strange behavior, she sank into a chair beside the kitchen table. She stared at her hands for some time. They were trembling.

"Mr. Concannon," she said quietly, "I have an uneasy feeling that I am going to begin screaming any minute if you don't tell me the meaning of all this."

Concannon sat at the table, looked at the whiskey bottle but didn't touch it. "We had to get away from the depot in a hurry. There wasn't time to explain."

"Why did we have to get away?"

He half-smiled and shook his head. "You're not goin' to believe it, but I think Bone was set to kill you."

"Why," she asked incredulously, "would a police officer want to kill me?"

"Because you're the loose thread in Bone's pattern—because of you his whole scheme is apt to unravel. He can't allow that."

Her face was strained. "Would you please tell me what you're talking about and what it has to do with Ray?"

Concannon took a deep breath. The time had come to tell her that her husband was a thief and a murderer. And, because it could not be put off any longer, he told her everything he knew.

For what seemed like a long time she merely stared at him, saying nothing, her eyes as eerily blank as they had been when he had seen her placing flowers on Ray's grave. At last she said in a hoarse whisper, "He's alive! Ray's alive! Are you sure?"

"Yes ma'am, I talked to him."

"But you're wrong about the robbery."

"No ma'am. He admitted it."

Annie opened the connecting door and looked at them. "There's ribs and biscuits in the oven, if you're hungry."

"Thanks, Annie. After a while, maybe."

Again Miss Annie Bee closed the door and left them alone. Athena was lost in her swirling thoughts. Several times she looked at Concannon and started to speak, but at the last moment changed her mind and said nothing. Little by little she was piecing the truth together for herself.

Concannon decided that he had shown enough restraint for one day and reached for the whiskey bottle. The silence in the small room became oppressive. The shade of Ray Allard sat between them at the table, grinning. "Me and Miss Annie Bee go back almost ten years," Concannon said abruptly to fill the silence. "She had a little end-of-track place in the Choctaw country. Some highbinders had it in mind to take over her business, and I managed to discourage them. That was when I was ridin' for the court at Fort Smith. Annie and I've kind of been pals since then." After a moment he added regretfully, "But I guess we won't be any more."

Athena did not look at him or hear him or give any indication that she even knew that he was in the room. What desperate thoughts were in her mind, Concannon could only guess.

He poured himself a stiff drink of Annie's whiskey. It was whiskey to take the hide off an Arkansas hog, but he drank it down as if it were water.

Suddenly Athena asked in a toneless voice, "Is he hurt?"

"He's been laid up," Concannon told her, "but he'll be all right. Bone's been lookin' out for him."

"I want to see him."

Concannon had been expecting this. He was ready to promise her anything to keep her quiet. "All right, I'll take you. But we'll have to wait a little."

"How long?"

"The first thing I've got to do is to see if my suspicions about Bone are right."

"How could they be right?" she demanded. "How could a policeman even think of killing anybody, much less a woman, on the streets in broad daylight?"

"Bone could do it. He could say he was shootin' at me—for any of a hundred reasons—and pass it off as an accident." He took another drink of Annie's whiskey. "You *don't* know anything about that robbery, do you?"

She looked at him with cool, dull eyes. "Is that what you've been thinking? That sooner or later I would tell you where the money is?"

"No ma'am, I never thought that for a minute." Then he said, "He's not worth all the worry and bother and tears and grief. I never should have told he was alive."

"No," she said sharply. It was almost a cry. "You did right. Because I don't really care what he has done, or what kind of man he is. He's alive. That's the only thing I can think of, the only thing I care about."

There seemed to be nothing to say after that. Outside they could hear the subtle change of sounds as daylight became dusk and dusk became the beginning of night-fall. Annie opened the door and said, "You want me to light a lamp?"

"No," Concannon told her, "we'll be leavin' before long."

"I sent some boys to sniff around and see could they find out about Bone. He's lookin' for you, Concannon. And her too." She shot a brief, curious glance at Athena Allard. "He's lookin' hard."

Concannon smiled grimly. "Give us an hour, Annie. We'll be gone by then."

Gone where? The only place he could think of was the Day and Night, and that would not be safe. It was sure to be the first place Bone would think of looking. Anyway, he wasn't at all sure that Lily would take them in.

"Well," he said after a long silence, "at least we know one thing for sure. Bone is convinced that you and Ray intend to double-cross him." It was not a comfortable thought to dwell on, but Athena did not look particularly frightened. Her thoughts were with Ray again.

Night came down on Oklahoma City. It did not steal in quietly, as it did in other places, it arrived with the thudding of a Salvation Army drum, the blare of a cornet and the rattle of a tambourine.

CHAPTER 11

The kitchen was dark now and the activity in the front part of the house was becoming more insistent. Miss Annie Bee, with the air of a woman who had settled her debt in full, opened the door. Concannon said, "We're just leavin', Annie. We're much obliged for your help."

"I haven't helped you. I haven't even seen you. Remember that if Bone gets his hands on you." She opened the back door and quickly looked up and down the dark alley. "It's all right. Good luck, Concannon. Same to you, ma am."

Expertly, Annie eased them through the doorway. She closed the door firmly after them. They heard her throw the bolt.

Concannon took Athena's hand. "There's a place I know—I think you'll be all right there."

She showed no sign of anxiety. "When can I see Ray?"

"Not till I have a chance to do a little scoutin'."

"Tonight?"

"As soon as I can manage it. Now watch your step." They made their way cautiously through dark alleyways and along dirt paths, angling generally toward the energetic thumping of the Salvation Army drum. Several voices, most of them slurred with liquor, were raised in song.

They crossed Bunco Alley near Front Street and approached the Day and Night from the rear. One of Lily's girls was out on the back porch, taking a minute for herself. Concannon said, "It's me, Peg. Concannon. Ask Lily if she can see me for a minute, will you?"

The girl made a startled sound and squinted in the darkness. "Concannon, don't you know Bone's lookin' for you?"

"I know. He's not in there now, is he?"

"A little while ago, but not now. He's accusin' you of robbin' a train and shootin' somebody and I don't know what all."

Concannon smiled thinly. That was Bone. Never do anything halfway. "Go and get Lily, and don't say anything."

In a few minutes Lily Olsen appeared in the doorway with Satan in her arms and a thin black cigarillo in her mouth. She came down the back steps and gazed steadily at Concannon and Athena. "Well," she drawled, "you got yourself in a fine fix this time. Bone's fit to be tied. I've never seen him so mad. I think he's mad enough to kill."

"So do I," Concannon told her. "Lily, can you put Mrs.

Allard up for a little while, till I do some scoutin'?"

"Bone's already turned the place upside down lookin' for you. I can't do anything to help you if he comes back." She looked at Athena. Her eyes, in the filtered lamplight, looked almost as yellow as Satan's. "You better go up the outside stairway," she told Concannon. "One of my girls, Dolly Woodruff, is takin' the night off. Mrs. Allard can stay in her room."

Concannon nodded toward the wooden ladder nailed to the side of the Day and Night. All such places took care to provide escape routes for the benefit of sensitive patrons wanting to leave in a hurry, in the unlikely event of a police raid. "Do you think you can climb the ladder all right, ma'am?"

"Were you a friend of my husband's?" Athena asked Lily Olsen.

"No, ma'am," Lily told her coolly. "I knew him, but we weren't friends." She shifted arms with Satan and stood out of the lamplight watching Concannon and Athena climb the outside stairway. She studied Athena closely and was bewildered when she discovered that the widow Allard was something less than a stunning beauty. Somehow she expected more of the woman who could derail Marcus Concannon.

Lily went back into the Day and Night and met them at the top of the stairs. "Here's the room," she said, nodding toward an open door. "It's not much; Dolly's not the best housekeeper I ever saw."

Athena allowed Concannon to take her arm and lead her into the room. It was more like a cell than a room.

185

There were no windows, and it smelled of carbolic acid. The only furniture was a bed, an oak wardrobe, and a washstand. Athena looked at the room without actually seeing it. "I want to see Ray tonight," she told Concannon.

The statement startled Lily Olsen. She set Satan down in the hallway and looked hard at Concannon. "What's this about Ray?"

Concannon hesitated only a second. He couldn't lie to Lily now; too much depended on her. "Ray got himself shot in the robbery, and Bone has been takin' care of him."

Lily's eyes were wide and unblinking. "Who did they bury in Ray's grave?"

With profound weariness, Concannon went through the story again. Lily thought about it for a moment, puffing on her cigarillo. She looked with new interest at Athena Allard. "So now Bone's convinced that Ray and Mrs. Allard are out to double-cross him?"

Concannon nodded. "That's the way it looks."

"With a hundred thousand dollars in the balance," Lily said coldly. "Yes, I can understand that Marvin Bone would murder for that kind of money. I can't say," she added, "that I'm right happy to get caught in the middle."

"Just for a little while, Lily."

She smiled ruefully. "For a little while. But what good will it do? You can't go to the police for help. You could never make them believe that Marvin Bone is prowling the streets lookin' to murder you and Mrs. Allard."

186

"They would listen to John Evers, if I can find him."

Lily cocked her head thoughtfully. "Maybe. I wouldn't want to gamble on it. But maybe." With a chilly little smile she nodded to Athena Allard, took Satan in her arms again and went down the stairs.

Concannon closed the flimsy door and bolted it. Downstairs they could hear the clatter of the wheel of fortune, the rattle of dice, the whoops of laughter. But there in Dolly Woodruff's shabby little cubicle Concannon and Athena Allard were in another world.

"Why don't you sit down?" Concannon said quietly. "Try to rest. I won't be long."

Obediently she sat on the edge of the bed. Dolly Woodruff's workbench. If she knew what kind of room she was in it didn't seem to disturb her. "He's alive," she said in wonder. "That's the only thing I can think of."

Concannon shifted feet uncomfortably. "Are you goin' to be all right here?"

She nodded.

"Then I guess I better go." Somehow he had to get to Evers. Evers represented the railroad, and the railroad represented power. City officials respected power. But what was he going to say to Evers when and if he found him? He didn't know—but it would have to be convincing. The grass money was the key. The board members wanted that money, and what the board members wanted, John Evers got for them. Maybe he could make a deal with Ray—exchange that money for his life. Maybe. But he didn't really believe it.

To Athena he said, "Try not to worry about Bone.

187

You'll be safe enough here."

She looked at him, surprised. She hadn't been thinking of Bone at all. For a moment she looked blank, not even remembering who Bone was. Concannon sighed to himself. When it came to making Marcus Concannon feel like a fool, Athena Allard had no equal. He reached for the door and said, "I won't be long."

But he didn't open the door. There was something in the air, an electricity that made his skin prickle. He was aware of an uneasy hush in the downstairs part of the Day and Night. Then Lily Olsen hollered indignantly, "You can't go upstairs, Bone! All my girls are busy!"

Concannon heard Bone answer with a curse. There was a brief scuffle. A table was overturned, poker chips clattered on the bare floor. Lily continued to holler, not so much in anger but as a warning to Concannon. Then there was the tramping of Bone's heavy brogans on the stairway, and Concannon thought, Nothing short of death can stop him now!

To Athena he said quickly, "Get up. Take off your dress."

She looked blank, then color flooded her face. "Quick," Concannon snapped. "There's no time to waste."

Surprisingly, she understood him completely. Within a matter of seconds, by the time Bone was halfway up the stairs, she had debated it in her mind and decided that it was necessary. By that time she was on her feet. Concannon slipped behind the heavy wardrobe. His double-action .38 was in his hand.

An instant before Bone kicked the flimsy door open, Athena Allard grasped the hem of her dress and pulled it over her head. That was how Marvin Bone found her, bent over, directly in front of the door, with her skirts over her head. She shrieked as the door flew open.

Immediately behind Bone, an enraged Lily Olsen was scratching at the policeman and raising a fearful commotion. Bone stood for a moment, glaring savagely. Then, with a snarl, he moved on to Peg Moore's door and kicked it open. There was another shriek. The scene was repeated three times. Bone broke into every room on the second floor, including Lily's living quarters.

Lily continued to holler at the top of her voice. She moved behind Bone, slamming the doors shut on the indignant girls and their unnerved customers. When she came to Dolly Woodruff's room she shot a look at Athena Allard—amusement mingled with relief and admiration. She grinned fleetingly at Concannon as he came out from behind the wardrobe. Then she closed the door.

Her face strangely pale and expressionless, Athena rearranged her clothing. On the other side of the door the storm still raged.

Marvin Bone bellowed his frustration. "I know they're here! Concannon and the Allard woman. Somebody saw them!"

"Somebody's lyin'!" Lily Olsen hollered. "I'll have your badge for this, Sergeant! Don't think I won't!"

Bone told her with carefully chosen obscenity what he thought of the threats of a whorehouse keeper. Threats and counterthreats flew like bullets, but in the end Bone had to admit defeat. He tramped back down the stairs, shaking the building in his rage. Only then did Concannon put away his revolver.

Within a matter of minutes the wheel of fortune began to chatter again. The dice rattled. The faro dealer readied his layout. It was business as usual at the Day and Night.

"Are you all right?" Concannon asked.

Athena's face was still pale but she managed a faint smile. "I'm all right." She shook her head. "I don't think I quite believed it before—but he would have killed us, wouldn't he?"

"Sergeant Bone is a man who's almost got his hands on a hundred thousand dollars. There's not much he won't do now to anybody that gets in his way."

For a moment there was terror in her eyes. "Ray!"

"Don't worry about Ray," Concannon told her dryly. "As long as he's the only one who knows where he hid the money he's the safest man in Oklahoma."

Concannon opened the door and glanced up and down the hallway. The girls had gathered in Peg Moore's room and were chattering indignantly, their nervous customers having long since shinnied down the rear stairway. "Bolt the door when I'm gone," he told Athena. Not that the bolt had stopped Marvin Bone or was likely to stop him the next time if he returned. Well, there was no profit in worrying about that now. He went quickly to the end of the hall and descended the ladder to the ground.

"Now ain't that a right considerate thing for you to do?" said Detective Sergeant Marvin Bone in delight.

"Climbed right down that ladder into my hands."

The policeman stepped out of a black shadow, his teeth gleaming yellow in the diffused light from the Day and Night. Concannon stared at that grinning face and a strange sense of fatalism took hold of him. There seemed to be no way of beating Bone; he discovered that he was tired of trying. He merely stood and watched Bone come toward him.

The sergeant chuckled. "Yes, sir, Concannon, right accommodatin' of you, I call it. I don't know what you and Allard's woman are schemin' but it don't make any difference now. You're dead, Concannon. Unless you get the woman down here right now, I'll kill you."

Concannon stared at the heavy .45 in the sergeant's hand. "Don't be a fool, Bone. She doesn't know anything about that money."

"I'll be the one to decide that. Get her."

Something happened inside Concannon's head. He saw himself laid out in the alleyway next to the Day and Night, his face battered, his ribs stove in. That had been Bone's doing. He saw himself riding peacefully over a rolling countryside—then two assassins bent on shooting him out of the saddle. More of Bone's doing. Suddenly he decided that he had had enough of Detective Sergeant Marvin Bone. Enough of his threats and spying and scheming. To the policeman's astonishment, Concannon threw himself at that casually held .45.

The revolver bellowed in the empty darkness. Concannon felt as if he had collided with the blunt side of an ax. He began to fall.

A single small, hot star burned in the dense darkness. For a brief time it burned intensely, then it waned, then it burned intensely again. It seemed to wink at Concannon. It changed its position slightly in the endless blackness. It floated, bobbed, and weaved there in its black infinity.

It seemed to Concannon that a great deal of time passed, but that single star remained constant, unchanging. The star and Concannon, alone in the blackness. They had the universe all to themselves.

Then suddenly the star glowed hotly. And it spoke. "You're not hurt, Concannon. Get up. The bullet barely grazed you."

The star burned furiously for a short time. Then once again it cooled. It smelled strongly of fine Cuban tobacco. Concannon was lying on his back, next to the Day and Night's rear steps, staring up at the flowing tip of John Evers's cigar.

Two strong, well-cared-for hands came out of the darkness, grasped Concannon's shoulders and hauled him to his feet. "Everything's all right," the inspector was saying casually to the wide-eyed faces at the saloon's back door. "Just a little accident. No trouble at all."

Lily Olsen clattered down the steps. "What's goin' on here?" She paled when she saw the blood on Concannon's face.

All the time John Evers was making soothing sounds and steering Concannon up the alley toward Front Street. Lily's voice went shrill. "I said, what's goin' on here! Somebody answer me!"

"Everything's perfectly all right, Miss Olsen," Evers assured her in a fatherly tone. "Just a little accident."

"Accident!" She circled them like an excited terrier, snapping and snarling. "Look at him! He's bleedin' to death! He's been shot!"

"Take my word for it, Miss Olsen, he isn't hurt. But he may be in trouble. You'd be doing him an important service if you returned to your establishment and quieted everybody down."

"Bring him into the Day and Night; I'll look after him."

"No," John Evers told her firmly, "that would not be wise."

"Who was it shot him!" Lily almost screamed. "Was it Bone?"

The inspector sighed. "Please, Miss Olsen, do as I say. It's best for everybody. Most of all, it's best for Concannon."

Concannon could just hear the shouting through the roaring in his head. His mouth was gritty and dry; his tongue felt as if it belonged to someone else. Several times he tried to speak, but a croaking, froglike sound was the best he could do. He leaned heavily on Evers. Patiently he practiced shaping words with his mouth. When he was confident that he could do it, he spoke.

"Lily. I'm all right. Do like Evers says. Look out for Athena Allard."

She stared at him. "At a time like this, all you can think about is Athena Allard!"

Blood soaked the side of Concannon's head and dripped from the point of his chin. He made himself grin. "Sorry, Lily. I have to do it my way."

"Your way almost got you killed just now."

"Lily."

She threw up her hands in anger. "All right, go on and get yourself killed. For a woman that don't even care if you're alive."

She wheeled and returned to the Day and Night, herding the curious customers back inside.

Concannon took a few practice steps on his own. His legs were rubbery, his head pounded like a Salvation Army drum, but he consoled himself with the thought that he was lucky just to be alive. Painfully, he turned his attention to John Evers and tried to focus his thoughts. "Where did you come from?"

"That's a long story," the inspector said wearily. "Can you walk all right?"

"I guess."

"Then let's go to the depot."

It was easier to go than to argue about it. Concannon allowed himself to be steered through the sparse clutter of animals and rigs. They entered the depot through the baggage room and eventually reached the sooty little cubicle that passed as Evers's office when he was in Oklahoma City.

From a drawer of his yellow oak desk Evers took out a bottle of Kentucky bourbon and a slightly soiled glass. "One glass is all I've got," he said, filling it to the brim and handing it to Concannon. Concannon drank some of the whiskey. It was so smooth that he could hardly feel it hit his stomach. A perfect match for Evers's Cuban coronas. He turned the glass up and drained it.

Evers refilled it. This time Concannon poured some of the whiskey on his handkerchief and dabbed at his bloody face. He winced when he touched the shallow scalp wound over his left ear. He drank the rest of the whiskey in the glass and said, "What happened to Bone?"

"Lit out. I guess he thought he'd killed you. So did I, at first."

"You saw it happen?"

"It was dark, but I saw it. I was about fifty yards up the alley, toward Front Street."

"You just happened to be standin' there, I guess, figgerin' that sooner or later somethin' interestin' would happen?"

Evers smiled. "I was sure something interesting would happen, if I followed Bone long enough."

The whiskey had soothed Concannon's stomach, but his head was pounding. "Let's start at the beginnin'. Why were you trailin' Bone? What were you doin' in the alley?"

Evers looked thoughtfully at the tip of his cigar. "The trouble with men like you, Concannon, is that you don't understand the pressures of responsibility. I am responsible for recovering one hundred thousand dollars of the railroad's money. If I don't recover it I'm apt to be out of a job, just as you are." He spread one hand on his knee and inspected his manicured nails. "I like my job. I don't intend to lose it. I am prepared to go to almost any length not to lose it. Perhaps this will explain to you why I sent the note."

"The note?" Concannon scowled, and that was a mistake—it only increased the pounding in his head.

"The note to Athena Allard." Evers smiled comfortably and puffed his cigar. "I'm sorry to say it, Concannon, but I can no longer trust you. As much as it goes against the grain, I had to resort to trickery." He beamed. "And it worked."

Concannon licked his dry lips. "You wrote that note to Athena?"

"Of course. And enclosed the money. And the train ticket. You remember the money, don't you? The two thousand dollars that you took from Mrs. Allard and gave to me to put in the safe? On the spur of the moment I thought about it—it made the note quite convincing, don't you think?"

"The note was in Ray's hand," Concannon objected. "Even Athena recognized it."

But Evers was shaking his head. "Forged. I had plenty of samples of Allard's handwriting, in his company reports. It was a simple matter—anyway, very few people remember what a person's handwriting looks like, except in a general way."

Concannon's mouth fell open, but all he said was, "Why?"

"I thought I'd explained that. I want that money. And, as I said, I could no longer trust you to get it for me. But somewhere along the line I got to thinking about Ab

Miller, the nitroglycerin expert. He, according to every-thing we knew, ought to have been the key to the matter. But Miller was nowhere to be found. Miller had disap-peared, as though he were dead." The inspector tapped an ash from his cigar. "Dead. Then do you know what I began to wonder, Concannon? I began to wonder about that body in Ray Allard's casket. It's Miller, isn't it?"

When Concannon made no reply, Evers shrugged. "It's Miller, all right, but I didn't know it then, I was only guessing. So I wrote the note. Mrs. Allard did just as I figured she'd do, she went to you for help. And Bone did as I figured *he* would do, he followed her. When he found out what was in the note he figured that she and her husband were double-crossing him, and . . ." He waved his cigar casually. "I think he would have killed her, if he'd had the chance. Just as he was about to kill you. But that was of no great importance to me." He paused, then asked abruptly, "Bone and Ray are in this thing together, aren't they?"

Concannon sat back and listened to the pounding in his head. He could feel the ground giving way beneath his feet.

"The way I see it," Evers continued, "is that Bone somehow blundered onto Ray's scheme and voted him-self a partnership. If Ray's alive it means that Bone doesn't yet know where the money is. And he's alive, because Bone believed what I had written in that note. And he believed that Ray had written it. So there we are. If anybody wants that money more than I do, it must be Bone. All I had to do was follow him and sooner or later he would lead me to Ray." For a moment he looked blank. Then he shook his head sadly. "It was an excellent plan. Unfortunately, even excellent plans have a way of going off the track."

Concannon stared at him. "Where was it derailed?"

John Evers had smoked a little more than half of his cigar and it was beginning to turn bitter. He dropped it to the floor and forgot it. "It was derailed," he said, "when you killed Bone. I'm afraid I didn't tell you the truth when I said that Bone ran away after the scuffle. He was in a rage, he meant to kill you. You must have known that in the back of your mind, even after the first bullet grazed your head."

Concannon heard himself asking, "The first bullet?"

"There were two shots. The one that hit you, and the one in the brief struggle that followed, as you were going down. It wasn't loud. The muzzle was turned to Bone's chest when it went off."

Concannon remembered nothing. Only the long fall into the bottomless pit. "If Bone is dead, where is the body?"

"Under the back steps of the Day and Night. I rolled it there before anybody saw it."

Concannon could think of only one word. "Why?"

"Because," Evers said, "if all my guessing has been correct, you and Bone were the only ones left who knew about Ray. Now there's only you. And I want you to tell me."

"How do you figure you'll get me to do that?"

For a moment the inspector's face went slack. He

looked tired. Concannon was surprised to realize that John Evers was an old man, despite his drive and trim, well-groomed appearance. An old man—but no less dangerous for that. "You'll tell me," Evers said, "because eventually I'll find out anyhow. And, if you don't cooperate now, I'll implicate Athena Allard. If it's the last thing I do I'll convince a jury that she and her husband were partners in that robbery."

Concannon felt as if the blood had stopped flowing in his body. "Does your job mean that much to you?"

Evers sat back in his chair, his eyes almost closed. "It does."

"What about Bone?"

"Self-defense. I'll swear to it, if you cooperate. And the railroad, with its hundred thousand dollars back in the bank, will support me."

Concannon hesitated, but only briefly. There was no reason for debate, no grounds for argument. John Evers held all the cards. "Are you goin' to arrest him?"

"There's no getting away from that now."

"I know Ray. I don't think he'll tell you where the money is."

Evers smiled, but his eyes were faded and empty. "He'll tell. There are ways."

"I want to talk to him before you take him."

The inspector shrugged. "That will be all right. Where is he?"

A scene as sharp as an ice etching flashed in Concannon's mind—Athena placing flowers on her husband's grave. "He's in a little rundown shack that

Bone had. Over by the Frisco freight house."

Evers nodded and smiled his satisfaction. Then Concannon startled him by suddenly laughing. It was a harsh, empty sound in that shabby little room. "Just a few minutes ago," Concannon explained, "I was tellin' Athena Allard that everything was going to be fine. Because I was going to find John Evers and he was going to help us."

CHAPTER 12

Concannon and Evers and two uniformed police officers arrived at the freight house in a police hack. Evers looked doubtfully at the dark shack half-hidden in the weeds. "Are you sure he's there?"

"He's wounded; he couldn't leave if he tried."

They left the team in the freight yard. The two policemen drew their revolvers and moved noisily through the dry weeds. When they were in place, guarding the rear of the shack, Concannon and Evers started up the dirt path.

"Wait here," Concannon said. "I won't be long."

"You've got ten minutes, then the policemen go in after him."

Concannon went up the path alone. The last time, he thought, Bone had been with him. Now Bone was dead. Turk and Croy were dead. So was Maggie Slatter and the pimp. And Ab Miller, and the clerk in that Santa Fe mail car. All because Ray Allard had got tired of trying to live on his lawman's pay.

He knocked on the door. "Ray, it's me, Marcus."

It seemed to Concannon that the night held its breath. Then: "Come on in, it ain't locked."

Concannon eased the door open and stepped inside. "All right to light the lamp?"

"Light it."

It took a minute for Concannon to locate the lamp in its wall bracket beside the door. Then he struck a match and saw Ray sitting up in bed, his face as pale as tallow in the sulphurish glare. There was a .45 revolver on the bunk beside him.

Concannon lit the lamp, he adjusted the wick, then he turned and the two men looked at each other for several seconds. At last Ray sagged back against a folded blanket. "You didn't come by yourself, did you?"

"No. John Evers and two policemen are outside."

Allard didn't look surprised. He looked too sick and too weak to express emotion. "How'd you manage to come here without Bone seein' you?"

"Bone's dead."

This did seem to surprise Allard. His eyes widened and he nodded his head several times as Concannon told him about the shooting. "Well," he said at last, "Bone wasn't much account, but I hate to lose him. He was all the help I had." He managed a faint, bitter smile. "I should of let him kill you, Marcus. Now it's too late. You're turnin' your old pal in to the law. Never mind the old days, when Ray Allard saved your life."

"I didn't have a choice, Ray. Evers was beginnin' to figure it out. He had already guessed that Bone was in it with you, he was just waiting for Bone to lead him to this shack."

"But the thing that matters is, it was my old pal that turned me in."

"Evers threatened to swear to a jury that you and your wife were partners in the robbery. You wouldn't want that, would you?"

"Nobody asked me what I wanted."

It was going even worse than Concannon had expected. Why had he come anyway? There was nothing to be done, no way to make the situation any easier. But he could try. "Ray, this is the only way. I don't know what a jury will do to you, but I do know you're goin' to die if you stay here. The bullet hole in your belly has gone rotten; you can smell it the minute you step through the doorway. But with a doctor lookin' after you, you've still got a chance."

"Chance for what? The hangman?"

"A chance to fight. There are good lawyers here in the Territory. Evers will help you, if you cooperate. And your wife . . . she's on your side."

"My wife . . ." Ray's eyes lost their focus. He looked blankly into space, thinking thoughts that Concannon could only guess at.

"Tell them where the money is, Ray. It can't help you now. But Evers is ready to help you, if he gets that money back."

Ray's eyes slowly cleared. He lay back on the folded blanket, managing a weak smile, and Concannon sensed that somewhere in that feverish brain a decision had been made. "Maybe you're right," he sighed. He made a meaningless gesture with one hand. "What good is that money goin' to do me now?"

"It could mean the difference between livin' and dyin'," Concannon said quickly.

"Do you know where the trestle is?" Ray asked slowly, carefully forming each word in his mind before putting it into sound. "About a mile north of the place where we stopped the train?"

"I know the place."

"That's where it is. Wedged in between the crossties and the first support member." With what seemed to be his last strength he laughed feebly. "Surprises you, some, don't it, that I'd tell?"

As a matter of fact, Concannon was surprised, but he merely said, "It was the only smart thing to do."

There was something in Concannon's words that seemed to amuse the dying man. He lay for a while, smiling—but after a time that too grew tiresome, and he sagged back on the bunk. "Now you've got what you wanted, and I'm sick of lookin' at you. Get out."

"I'm sorry, Ray."

"Get out," he said again, his voice hissing.

So this is the way it ends, Concannon thought numbly. After all the years together. All the black nights and long rides and the danger. He said heavily, "So long, Ray." He turned and reached for the door.

Suddenly a breath as cold as death raised the hairs on the back of his neck. A prickling warning, born of a thousand days of living with danger, raced over the surface of his skin. It was not a thing to be thought about and pondered on, it was to be acted on immediately or not at all. He wheeled away from the door an instant before it was violently splintered by the slug from Ray's .45.

The next second passed with nightmarish slowness. The picture of Ray holding the heavy .45 in both hands, his face twisted with rage, the cloud of gunsmoke in the air—it was all etched with acid in Concannon's brain. It required no thought or evaluation. Everything was chillingly clear. *Ray was trying to kill him.*

And now Concannon understood why Ray had told him about the money. He hadn't meant for it to matter one way or the other. It had been his final little joke, for it had never been in his mind for Concannon to leave the shack alive.

The fact that his light, blunt little double-action .38 had somehow moved from his shoulder holster to his right hand did not surprise Concannon. It was a matter of training, and the instinct to survive. The small weapon bellowed, a sound of ear-splitting violence. For an instant his thoughts were amazingly clear. His finger was taut on the trigger, but he did not fire a second time. For several seconds he did nothing at all but stand there watching Ray's pale, twisted face through the curtain of gunsmoke.

With a little sigh Ray Allard fell over on his side. His heavy .45 clattered to the floor. His eyes were wide open and staring and quite dead.

The door burst open and the two policemen rushed into the shack, with John Evers just behind them. Evers stared for a moment at the dead man on the bunk. His face turned red, his eyes glittered like broken glass. "You fool!" he shouted at Concannon. "You killed him! He was the only one who could tell me where the money is!"

Marvin Bone, in a way that he had not foreseen, finally made good on his threat to show Concannon the inside of the "Cottonwood de Bastile." For seven days nervous and angry police officials had questioned him on the death of Bone. It had not been a pleasant experience. Then one day the turnkey threw open the door with an ingratiating grin. "It pays to have pals in high places, don't it, Concannon?"

Concannon regarded the open door with disbelief. "I'm free?"

"The city council wants you out of the Territory before sundown—that's all I know."

John Evers met him in the basement police headquarters where Concannon reclaimed his personal belongings. "Is this your doin'?" Concannon asked uncertainly.

Evers shrugged. "For five years you were a first-class railroad agent. I guess the company owes you this much." He selected a perfect corona from his cigar wallet and sniffed it appreciatively. "Anyway, the testimony I gave to the officials was true. You killed Bone in self-defense." Suddenly he smiled. "Frankly, they weren't too eager to prosecute. Man like Bone—touchy business. Might throw a bad light on the whole force."

"Much obliged for your help, Mr. Evers."

"Goodbye, Concannon."

They did not shake hands. After a moment Concannon nodded, turned away and left.

That afternoon a uniformed policeman escorted Concannon to the depot and saw that he bought a ticket on the next northbound out of the Territory. The policeman's name was O'Doul—he was big and young and looked as if he might be reasonably honest.

While Concannon and O'Doul were sitting on the iron-hard bench of the Santa Fe waiting room, a hack driver came in carrying a set of women's grips. Athena Allard followed him into the waiting room.

Instinctively, Concannon started to lurch to his feet. But there was something about her that froze him. She looked through him, as though he were invisible, and then she went to the ticket window and asked the agent for a ticket to her home in Kansas.

O'Doul watched this little drama with mild interest. He was aware that Concannon had been questioned for several days in the "Cottonwood de Bastile" because of the killing of Sergeant Bone. But in the end they had let Concannon go, on the unspoken recommendation of John Evers. A queer bird, O'Doul decided to himself, shooting the former railroad agent a curious glance. They said he'd been moon-eyed over Ray Allard's wife.

Well, the policeman thought, she sure wasn't moon-eyed over *him*. When she turned away from the ticket window and looked at Concannon for just a moment, there was an iciness in her eyes that made the young policeman's skin crawl. Then she went outside to wait beside her grips for her train.

"Officer," Concannon said after a long silence, "it doesn't really matter whether I go north or south, does it? As long as I get out of the Territory?"

The policeman thought about it and shrugged. "I guess not."

"Would you exchange these tickets for someplace in Texas? Then we'll go to a cafe and eat dinner and do our waitin' there."

This arrangement suited the young lawman fine. It wasn't every day that the man you were watching offered to buy you a meal.

They went to a cafe near the depot on Front Street, but Concannon couldn't eat. He drank a beer instead and watched O'Doul stoke himself with pigs knuckles and beans, and he tried not to think too much about Athena Allard.

The two o'clock northbound was on time. Concannon heard the whistle as it approached the switches. He heard the Baldwin huffing as it came to a stop in front of the depot. Athena will be boarding now, he thought. The porter will be handing up her grips. By this time tomorrow she will be at her folks' place in Kansas.

It might as well have been the moon.

He listened to the big Baldwin pulling out of the station. It worked hard, but steadily and uncomplainingly, as it mounted the north grade of the Canadian River Valley. After a while the sound of the locomotive became confused with the noises of the city—and then he could not hear it at all.

Concannon and his escort returned to the depot where the agent told them the next southbound was due at four o'clock. Concannon took a seat on a baggage cart, lit a cigar, and prepared to wait. He kind of wished that somebody would come to see him off. Lily, maybe. Or even John Evers.

But nobody came.

Center Point Publishing
600 Brooks Road • PO Box 1
Thorndike ME 04986-0001 USA

(207) 568-3717

US & Canada:
1 800 929-9108